The Chancery Murders

Josué Raúl Conte

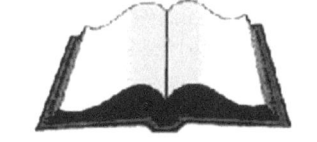

CCB Publishing
British Columbia, Canada

The Chancery Murders: Volume 2 of the Rosanada Trilogy

Copyright ©2009 by Josué Raúl Conte
ISBN-13   978-1-926585-33-8
Second Edition

Library and Archives Canada Cataloguing in Publication
Conte, Josué Raúl, 1969-
The chancery murders / written by Josué Raúl Conte. – 2nd ed.
(The Rosanada trilogy ; v. 2)
ISBN 978-1-926585-33-8
I. Title. II. Series:°Conte, Josué Raúl, 1969- . Rosanada trilogy.
PS3603.O5624C53 2009   813'.6   C2009-904114-6

Cover image ©2006 Jupiter Images Corporation www.clipart.com

Publisher: CCB Publishing
             British Columbia, Canada
             www.ccbpublishing.com

Volume 2 of

The Rosanada Trilogy

1

Renato

"Good morning, Josette."

"*Bonjour, monseigneur.* Your breakfast is ready in the dining room."

Wearing his bathrobe with his swim trunks underneath, Renato Del'Ano entered the dining room where Josette, the Haitian maid had laid out a bountiful buffet. Strangely, His Excellency Archbishop L'Abbadon was not already there eating, because he was usually the first one up in the morning. He must have had a late night, Renato mused, as he filled his plate with hot biscuits, scrambled eggs and bacon. Just as he was taking his place at the table, the archbishop entered the room looking haggard, quickly filled his plate, and sat down across from Renato.

"Where is Jan?" the prelate inquired impatiently. "He knows I have an important appointment this morning, and he is still not up. Have you seen him, Josette?"

"*Mais non, monsieur.*" She poured coffee into the bone china Haviland cups and then set the cream and sugar at the archbishop's right.

Obviously annoyed that Zagan was not there, he said to the maid, "Go, right away to his room and tell him to get down here at once." The archbishop sighed deeply, displaying his displeasure that his vicar general was still abed. Jan Zagan, an old friend since seminary days, frequently spent the night at the residence of the Archbishop of Rosanada, and was usually up on time for breakfast.

"I can always count on you, Renato. You are always punctual. That is important to me especially during these trying times when I have to discipline so many priests for their failure to keep their pants zipped up around young people, women seeking to be priests, and laypeople demanding accountability. The world has gone mad!" Renato watched as the archbishop spread butter and strawberry jam on a biscuit and began eating it.

When Josette returned a few minutes later, the archbishop's volatile temper was on the verge of exploding in a violent tirade when she told him, "He is not in his room. The bed has not been slept in."

Having quickly finished his breakfast, Renato announced, "I am going out to the pool for a swim. Don't worry. I won't be there long, and I will be on time to drive you to your morning appointment." After pouring a second cup of coffee, he took it and headed for the Olympic size pool that L'Abbadon had built behind the residence. He certainly was not prepared for what awaited him.

Renato screamed wildly as he discovered Jan

Zagan dead, floating in the water, buoyed up by the water wings he always wore in the pool, since he could not swim. There was something stuffed in his mouth between clenched teeth. As Renato drew near he could see that the vicar general's shorts had been ripped from his body and tossed on a chair by the pool where the monogram CAL– Cecil Anselm L'Ababdon, was clearly visible. Obviously, he had lost a lot of blood, judging from the condition of the water. As he drew nearer to where the vicar general was floating, he could see that his body had been mutilated; his penis had been severed with only a bloody stump remaining of his manhood. It was the severed member that was stuffed into the cavity of his mouth, where it had oozed blood that was now dry on the cheeks of the dead man. He had obviously been dead for some time.

Retching violently, Renato turned and made his way back to the dining room where the archbishop was just finishing his second cup of coffee.

"Jan Zagan," he announced somberly, "is in the pool."

"Tell him to get in here at once!" L'Abbadon commanded tapping his finger on the table for emphasis.

"Can't. He is dead."

"Did he have an accident?" the archbishop asked, stunned by the news.

Visibly shaking Renato answered, "I think someone killed him, cut off his penis and stuffed it in his mouth. I had better call the police."

"What a scandal this is going to be!" L'Abbadon moaned massaging his temples, as if he had a headache. "I should call the papal nuncio right away. Perhaps you will have to call the police," he spoke softly, as if out of respect for the dead Zagan. "Who would want to kill my vicar general?" Staring intently at his well manicured fingers and his star sapphire episcopal ring, he added. "Yes, I should call the nuncio first. Rome will instruct as how to proceed."

"We have no choice, Your Excellency; we must call the police at once. I'll take care of it." He whipped his cell phone from his bathrobe pocket and punched in 911. "Get me the police. There has been a homicide." A minute later when the detective came on the line, Renato gave him the address— seven Coziness Lane in Champs de Bauchery and described what he had seen in the pool. The homicide detective assured him that he would be on the scene within thirty minutes.

Renato was ready to take charge of the situation. They needed to keep calm. Quickly gulping a couple of Klonopin pills with a cup of sacramental wine, he hastened to respond to L'Abbadon's demand that he inject him with diazepam. He fumbled with the syringe that the archbishop kept always handy for times of stress and injected him with the strongest dose of diazepam available and gave him a jigger of Scotch to calm his nerves.

When the detective arrived, Renato met with him

in the drawing room where the candelabra were ablaze before the bigger than life painting of L'Abbadon. The detective was drinking in the opulence of the salon. Heavy brocaded drapes, imported Oriental carpeting, and black lacquered Chinese furniture, all indicated that the best decorators money could buy had furnished the room. The crystal chandelier looked like a museum piece. However, the thing that attracted the detective's attention was the great portrait of Archbishop L'Abbadon that reached from floor to ceiling. A pair of three branched golden Florentine candlesticks stood with one on each side of the portrait, giving the appearance of a sacred shrine. There he was in his entire formal magnificence— Cecil Anselm L'Abbadon —black cassock with cape all piped in fuchsia, with matching fuchsia buttons and brilliant fuchsia sash. He was even wearing fuchsia socks to match and had a fuchsia biretta on his shaggy gray head. His splendid pectoral cross studded with four diamonds, four rubies and four emeralds hung from his neck on a heavy gold chain.

Renato could see that the detective was carefully observing each detail of the painting. The archiepiscopal ring matched his pectoral cross; it was also in gold and contained matching gems. Carefully arranged on a chair beside the archbishop in the painting, but made to look as if it had been casually placed there, was a miter resplendent with many jewels —emeralds, rubies, and diamonds. Beside it were a glorious fuchsia floor-length cope and a mahogany crosier with a golden crook bearing his monogram CAL in emeralds, rubies and diamonds. Spotlights on the ceiling illuminated the portrait so that whenever anyone entered the room, their eyes were immediately attracted to the painting.

Renato observed the detective as he stood staring at the magnificence of His Excellency Cecil Anselm L'Abbadon who stood posed with one hand folded inside the other, and a big smile on his face, as if he were simply delighted with his munificent magnitude.

Amused at the impression that the portrait always made on those seeing it for the first time, Renato walked over to the detective and introduced himself.

"I am Monsignor Renato Del'Ano, the secretary to the archbishop," Renato said, as he extended his hand to the young detective whom he judged to be about forty years of age.

"Cristian Forte, Monsignor. Please take me to the scene of the crime, and then I will want to ask His Excellency a few questions. First my crew and I want to seal off the crime scene and photograph all the relevant details, including shots of the victim."

"But," protested Renato, taking an aggressive stance and confronting the detective, "he is naked and in a very compromising situation. We have to avoid a scandal. We can't have a photo of the dead and mutilated vicar general on the front page of the

Rosanada News. Those pictures will be in the public domain once they reach the district attorney's office. Then all the news media will have access to them." Renato cringed at the thought of Zagan's naked body being displayed on television and the press.

"I do understand your problem, but I have to follow police procedures. You might talk to the mayor to see if he can help keep this under wraps, but I doubt than any political influence will be able to keep a lid on this. Once this story hits the media, it will be all over the country within hours. You had better brace yourself and tell His Excellency to be prepared for the worst. No doubt Wayne Creasy will be sniffing around for the story, once it leaks out. You may also be assured that all TV channels will be here soon. I have to file a crime report for the records and the press will have access to it."

Renato trailed behind Forte as he directed his crew how to proceed at the crime scene. Yellow tape roped off the entire pool area with signs forbidding anyone to enter. Since Zagan's corpse was floating due to the water wings, it was easier to remove it from the pool than it would have been, if it had sunk to the bottom. Renato watched as they used a winch and a small crane to lift the blubbery, obese body of the vicar general from the water, noticing that there were contusions on his bull-like neck and torso.

"Can you identify him positively?" Forte asked.

"Yes, he is Jan Zagan, the Vicar General of the

Archdiocese of Rosanada."

"And the monogram on his shorts? CAL?

"Cecil Anselm L'Abbadon. Zagan spent the night here, probably borrowed a pair of shorts from the archbishop."

Forte directed his men to place the corpse in the homicide van parked at the side of the mansion. That done, he said, "Now I need to talk to the archbishop."

"Of course." Renato led the detective back into the archiepiscopal mansion and left him in the den and went to fetch the archbishop from his room, telling him that the detective insisted on talking to him personally.

"Yes, Renato, I will talk to the detective, but I want you to be present during the interview." After putting on a cassock and his pectoral cross in an attempt to elevate himself above the police, L'Abbadon made his way to the den where Forte was waiting.

"Good morning, Your Excellency," Forte began, extending his hand to the archbishop. I need to ask you some questions."

L'Abbadon remained silent, looking at the detective with distrust written on his freckled face. He was a tall man with extremely very fair skin, a full head of white hair and a very prominent nose, making him reminiscent of Jean Cocteau. Although he had a deep and mellow voice, it could become quite harsh and strident, when he was crossed. Then his facial expression would darken, as he clenched his teeth and the corners of his mouth drooped downward. Renato was quick to notice that he was pursing his thin lips, contracting them into a circle— a characteristic facial expression when he was annoyed, stressed, or faked a smile for people he did not like.

"Any idea who might want to kill Jan Zagan?" detective Forte asked as he studied L'Abbadon's face intently.

"No idea at all, but it must have been someone who hated him very much."

"Do you have any contacts with the Mafia? This looks like a Mafia assassination."

Renato thought about Yo-Lin Sin and her Mafia friends, but said nothing.

"Look, Detective Forte, I know of no reason why the Mafia would want to kill Zagan."

"When was the last time you saw Zagan alive?"

"Last night. We played gin rummy until about eleven, and then I went up to bed. Zagan said he was going to take a dip in the pool before retiring. I knew he could not swim, but he always stayed in the shallow end, and always wore water wings to keep him afloat. That is the last I saw of him— alive."

Renato noticed that L'Abbadon had a tremor in his voice as he spoke and his hand shook slightly as he sipped the contents of a snifter of brandy.

"I have absolutely no idea of who could have done this horrible thing to Jan," L'Abbadon said forcefully.

"Did you and he get along well together?"

"Of course. He was my friend as well as my vicar general. We attended the university together in Rome. Been friends ever since.

Renato remembered the violent argument the two of them had the previous evening, but kept silent.

Detective Forte studied the faces of both Renato and the archbishop. "Have you had any problems with anyone? Have you fired anyone recently?"

L'Abbadon bristled and snapped, "Sir, if you would like to interrogate me, I will have to ask the archdiocesan lawyers to come immediately."

"We will let the questioning wait for now. But you will be interrogated," Forte responded.

"Set up an appointment with my lawyers Puck, Warhol and Associates. I will be glad to accommodate you."

Forte extended his hand to L'Abbadon, who had a cold and sweaty palm, and concluded the interview saying, "I don't have any suspects at the moment. I am sympathetic to you both. I am Catholic, and I even spent a year in a major seminary. I had always planned to be a priest all my life, but..." Detective Forte left the rest of the sentence unspoken and suddenly changed the subject. "Look, Archbishop, I don't want to worry you, but it just occurs to me that perhaps the killer was really after you. When it comes out in the papers that the vicar general was the man who was murdered, the killer might return looking for you. I can't caution you enough. Be very careful."

Renato observed that L'Abbadon shuddered and became quite pale as the detective voiced this warning. He, too, would have to be very careful. No doubt L'Abbadon had made many enemies. He had no intention of winding up in the pool like Zagan or perhaps meeting a worse fate.

2

L'Abbadon

His Excellency, the Most Reverend Cecil Anselm L'Abbadon, J.C.D., B.S.D., D.D, Archbishop of Rosanada, Grand Master of the Equestrian Order of the Most Holy Foreskin, Assistant to the Supreme Pontiff's Throne, and Pontifical Protector to the Tiberius Caesar Children's Choir uttered a deep sigh of relief when Forte shook his hand, took his leave, and hurried to join his crew that was waiting in the van to take the corpse of Jan Zagan to homicide headquarters where the autopsy was to be performed.

Quickly he reached again for a bottle, this time Courvoisier, that he kept in the liquor cabinet in the den and poured himself a substantial shot in his best French crystal snifter. As the fiery cognac began flowing through his veins, he felt fortified. The tremor was gone from his hand, but he was still agitated and worried. What if the police thought he had killed Jan! No doubt, he would be a suspect. Yet, Forte had said that he himself had probably been the one the killer was after. Who would want to kill him?

He had kept on good terms with Yo-Lin Sin and her friends in the Latino Mafia that always contributed so generously to his charities. However he *had* rebuffed her when she came to his office at the chancery the previous week. He recalled the cloying scent of her Oriental perfume that nauseated him when she threw her arms around him to embrace him, as she came tripping across his office to where he stood behind his massive mahogany desk that was meant to keep people always at a distance. Her dress, emblazoned with a gold brocaded dragon across the front, clung to her body revealing every sensuous detail. He could still remember how her silicon breasts pressed insistently against his chest and peeked out over the low-cut top of her jade green oriental tunic, attempting to entice him. Although he tried to conceal his true feelings toward her, perhaps he had offended her unwittingly. She was simply revolting to him, and he found that difficult to conceal.

"Well, Yo-Lin to what do I owe the pleasure of your visit?" He invited her to sit in the chair on the opposite side of his desk. He always felt more comfortable when his over-sized desk shielded him from women.

Before answering his question, she opened her large green alligator purse and, removing a gold cigarette case, pulled out an oval Egyptian cigarette and lit it with a matching gold lighter. Thoughtlessly, she blew the smoke in his direction, causing him to cough. Not seeming to notice that the acrid smoke was offensive to him, she smiled at him coyly and purred, "What a handsome office you have, Cecil. It really suits you. It is a powerful office—a place of power for a powerful man." She crossed her legs seductively and let her tunic slip several inches above her knees, but he pretended not to notice.

"So what can an archbishop do for such a charming woman?" he inquired biting his lip and completely unflustered by her feminine attractions.

"Rather, it is I who want to do something for you, Your Excellency."

He eyed her cautiously and waited for her to explain. "Perhaps you would like a glass of Port," he proffered. "I keep some here in my office for late afternoon visitors; I find it really comforting." He opened a cabinet next to his desk and removed a 40 year-old bottle of Garrafeira, a real treat for connoisseurs, and poured the deep purple wine into two French crystal glasses.

"Your taste is always superb!" she sighed, as she delicately sipped her drink. "I just stopped by to bring you a small check for your charities from me and my friends." Reaching inside her green alligator purse, she found the check and handed it to him across the desk."

In spite of the fact that she humiliated him by not placing it inside an envelope, he very discreetly took the check from her slender fingers, noticing that she wore an intricate jade ring on her right hand

and her nails were painted with jade enamel. As she rearranged an ivory comb that held her ebony hair in place, he took a quick glance at the check. It was a tidy sum—50K. He could not repress the pleased smile that crept across his face.

"My dear Yo-Lin, how thoughtful of you! This comes in handy for me to continue helping the needy." He thought of how he needed to refurbish his yacht and how it would probably take the entire amount.

"It is always my pleasure to assist you in your great charitable work." She took the last sip of port and placed the glass on his desk. "I am having a party in two weeks for my friends and we would be honored, if you would attend."

"Yes, of course. I would be delighted to come," he lied.

"It will be formal and I will send you an invitation. And one more thing," she hesitated a moment and then said, "My friends and I are very unhappy that you closed the Goretti Church Restoration Society that Monsignor Renato Del'Ano founded. Could you please reinstate it?" Her jade green eyes peered intently into his. "You remember, it was the St. Thomas Society before Monsignor changed its name."

Yes, he did remember. He remembered it well. Yo-Lin and her friends, namely, the Latino Mafia, had been using the society to launder their money, and he had felt it prudent to close it down. What a

15

fine scandal would that have made! He could imagine the headlines in the *Rosanada News.* "Rosanada Archdiocese launders money for the Mafia!" No thanks! He was not about to let them do that to him again. He pondered the matter for a few seconds and said, "I will see what I can do. I can't promise you anything, you understand. It would be very difficult to resuscitate that organization. All those that were involved with it have flown to the four winds. It would be very difficult indeed to resurrect it." He rose to his feet and extended his hand across the desk to shake hers, signifying that the meeting was at an end. Undaunted by this, Yo-Lin rushed around the desk and threw her arms around his neck. Again he felt an overwhelming sense of repugnance. As tactfully as he could, he withdrew from her embrace and walked her to the door of his office, opened it, and guided her out.

A few days later when the invitation arrived, he mailed her his acceptance, but when the time came for the party, he gave her a vague excuse to avoid attending. Surely the Mafia would not want him dead for that! Surely the Goretti Society did not mean that much to them. Perhaps they killed Jan just to let him know they were serious about doing business with him.

His thoughts of Yo-Lin and her fiends were interrupted by the jangling of the phone. It was Renato informing him that Kenneth Rafferty, the mayor of Rosanada, was on the other line.

"I'll take the call, Renato, put him on."

"Good day, Archbishop," the mayor greeted him. "I hear you had a bit trouble and I called. I thought I might be able to help." Kenneth Rafferty was a practicing Catholic and a politician to his very core. "I just heard that someone killed Jan Zagan. Such a good man, too. Rosanada will miss him. What can I do to help the Church?"

"Thanks for your call, Ken. I would like to keep this horrible affair as quiet as possible and avoid scandal. I have decided to celebrate the funeral services for Jan on Friday. I hope you will come and sit with the honored guests. The nuncio is coming down from Washington and many of the American cardinals have sent their condolences and have indicated they are coming to the Mass and interment."

"Of course, I will be there. You can count on me, Your Excellency, for anything you need, but it is next to impossible to keep a murder secret. It is not like fixing a traffic ticket. I'll see what I can do."

No sooner had the mayor got off the phone, when it rang again. This time it was Forte. "The medical team is working on the autopsy. We should have their findings by tomorrow noon. I need to ask you if you know of any reason the Mafia would want Zagan dead. I find it bizarre that his penis was raggedly chopped off and stuck in his mouth. That makes it sound to me either like an assassination by people in syndicated crime or a sado-masochistic sex

17

crime. If you get any insights into his murder, I ask you to call me at once.

"Of course, "L'Abbadon responded tersely with absolutely no intention of contacting him.

"I'll be in touch. Please, don't leave town." When the receiver clicked and the call ended, the archbishop summoned Renato, and when his secretary entered the den, he said quietly, "I am ready for you to drive me to the chancery. Jan is dead, but we will continue on with business as usual. We will, of course close the chancery the day of his funeral."

3
Forte

When he got the autopsy report on Jan Zagan, Cristian Forte was not surprised by what he learned. The amount of alcohol detected in his body was so high that he must have been completely tanked at the time of death, which was set at approximately eight or nine hours before he was discovered dead in the pool. His bloated body had many bruises, indicating a struggle, but of course, the sexual mutilation also suggested that Zagan might have been involved in sex play that got carried too far. Since the archbishop had stated that Zagan could not swim, it probably would have been easy in his drunken condition for someone to hold his head under water until he drowned. The autopsy listed the cause of death as drowning and loss of blood.

Obviously the Church was falling apart. He had wanted to be a priest all his life, ever since he was eight years old. He had even gone to the minor seminary, and on to the major seminar, but dropped out after one year, when he realized that the faculty members were almost all gay and none of them seemed to believe what the Church had taught down through the centuries. Liberal theology was touted and traditional belief was not tolerated. Instead of transubstantiation, his professors insisted that nowadays everyone believed in transignification. But he reasoned that if you throw out the Real Presence in the Eucharist, there is nothing left of the Catholic faith. No doubt that is why the professors in the seminary taught situation ethics. To them there were no fixed moral absolutes. Morality was determined by situations with no hard and set rules applied. Any act could be justified, if you tried. So he decided to become a cop. As a police officer, he knew where he stood with the law, and if people broke the law, their rationalization would not take their guilt away. You tracked down the guilty and brought them to justice.

His experience in the seminary had almost ruined his faith. What little that was left of it was tarnished by the pedophile scandals that racked the priesthood. He had been reared in a family of Italian and Puerto Rican origins that had moved from San Juan to the mainland of the United States and had settled in Rosanada, when he was about five years old. His parents were devout Catholics as were their friends who attended Santiago Church and were happy there until the pastor, Father Marco Lamadrid was falsely accused of sexual molestation and removed from his pastorate and an incompetent priest Clitor S. Del Sapo was sent to take over, causing the parish to sink into a state of disarray.

The present pastor Colin Olid had not yet been able to resurrect the parish, and probably never would, judging from his performance to date.

Forte realized that Father Marco was one of the people that he would have to interrogate about Jan Zagan's death. Since he had been in the archdiocese for thirty years and knew everyone, he might be able to give him some insights into the Zagan murder. Father Marco had built a new life for himself as a very successful Protestant pastor of a large nondenominational Pentecostal congregation in the south part of Rosanada.

Pulling into the driveway of his modest Cape Cod style home along the Rosanada River, Josue's heart sank. He hated coming home to an empty house. There was nothing sacred anymore. His marriage had crumbled a month ago, when his wife Anita had walked out on him, returning to her parent's house with Miguel, their eighteen year old son. Life had become very lonely, and he looked forward to the few hours he got to spend with his son every weekend.

His whole world had caved in. The Church that he relied on for faith had failed him. The murder at the archbishop's mansion was just one more proof of that. Without his wife and son, what was there to live for? Just his work and he was determined to find out who killed Jan Zagan and bring him to justice.

4
L'Abbadon

Unable to sleep L'Abbadon stared up from his bed at the ceiling of his room, covered with imported Venetian glass, in which he could see himself reflected, but found no satisfaction in what he saw. Although he had refrained from looking at the corpse when the police had taken him away, images of the mutilated Jan Zagan kept plaguing him. Why had someone so brutally severed his penis and stuffed it in his mouth? The horror of it all sent chills of fear racing down his spine. He tossed aside the lavender brocaded moiré silk bedspread that covered him and rose slowly to his feet.

Since he could not sleep, he decided to go into his private chapel that adjoined his bedroom. It had always been a place of peace for him, a sanctuary where no one was allowed to disturb him. The sight of his black Brazilian mahogany altar and the red candle flickering beside the tabernacle had always been a solace for him that spoke of peace and tranquility. The golden tabernacle flanked by ten golden candlesticks gave him a sense of deep satisfaction. Mounting his gilded archiepiscopal throne, also a Brazilian import, he took his place to the left of the altar.

No doubt Jan needed prayers. Quietly he mumbled a few Hail Marys for the repose of the vicar general's soul. It certainly wasn't his fault that Jan was killed right there on the grounds of the archiepiscopal mansion. He was above reproach. He had done nothing wrong. There was no guilt on his soul with which to reproach himself. He could justify all his actions—there was no sin in his life. Recalling the long time he had known Zagan—almost fifty years—he knew that the man had homosexual liaisons in the past. Thank God, Zagan had always been discreet and never got involved with any minors. However, he should never have made it a habit to visit gay bars. How many times had he reprimanded Zagan for that! Could one of his playmates have done this awful thing to him?

He thought of all the Mafia murders he had read about in the *Rosanada News*. He really never should have gotten mixed up with the Mafia, but his predecessors were the cause of that. The Mafia was well entrenched in the archdiocese, when he arrived on the scene. He would have to think of someway to get them off his back.

Forcing their way into his consciousness were the faces of all the priests he had removed from their parishes and put on administrative leave or defrocked. Although many protested their innocence, he had no qualms about getting rid of them. When he threatened them with a canonical trial, they all stopped protesting, knowing that it was useless to oppose him, for he had the power to do as he wished in the Rosanada Archdiocese. All of them had been accused and he had paid off all their accusers to silence them and avoid costly litigation in the courts where the Church would be subjected to scandal, and he would have to go on the witness stand and be subjected to intense questioning about all his activities since becoming archbishop. The very stupidity of a priest sexually abusing a young person appalled him. They all deserved the treatment he had given them.

Since he could not pray, except to recite a few vocal prayers, remaining in his chapel became wearisome to him, and he could find no peace for his tormented soul. Perhaps after they buried Jan on Friday, he would feel better. Today he would offer Mass for the repose of Zagan's soul, hoping that he himself would find peace.

Although he returned to his king-sized mahogany bed with his initials emblazoned in gold on its headboard, he was unable to fall asleep. His mind turned to all the parishes he had been forced to close because of dwindling attendance and lack of revenue. One church was sold and turned into a supper club. They kept the marble altar railing and used it as a divider between the restaurant and the bar. Out of the altar, they made some kind of side table or buffet for the restaurant. Every time he had to close a church, there were many angry people. He realized that they and their immigrant parents paid for many a church with quarters they managed to save from their limited earnings. Well if they did not meet their expenses and send a sizeable sum to his annual appeal, he could not afford to keep them open.

It was with very little regret that he closed Pope Julius III seminary. There just were not enough seminarians to justify keeping it open. So now it was a state prison and filled to capacity with the miscreant elements of society. It was a great irony that some of the men who had studied there to become priests were now incarcerated within its walls for their sexual crimes against minors.

It was not easy being an archbishop. He was bound to make enemies in all sectors of the Church. No doubt he even had enemies in the chancery too. He simply could not please everyone and satisfy them all. He had to show them who was boss. Once he got enough money together, he would take it to Rome on his *ad limina* visit and use it to buy influence in order to get a cardinalate. He wondered how much it would cost to do that. His predecessor had managed to make Rosanada an archbishopric years ago with his cash contributions, distributed with finesse in the right Roman hands.

When he finally fell asleep shortly before dawn, he dreamed that Pope Benedict XVI held a consistory and named him Cardinal of Rosanada. In triumph, he went to Rome and received the crimson hat. Soon, however, his dream changed. Rome vanished and he found himself in utter darkness. To his horror he was standing on an island in a lake of fire with the flames lapping at its shores. Then, suddenly, he realized that he was not alone. He saw Jan Zagan come running toward him. He knew he had to escape from his attempts to catch him. Zagan was naked and the bloody stump that had once been his pride and joy was bleeding profusely. Closer and closer he came with his arms and hands reaching out to him to grab his clothing and enslave him in their bloody embrace. When Zagan touched him, he awoke with a jolt and screamed.

Unable to go back to sleep, he got up, and dressed for the day ahead. Nothing he did brought him peace. As the day went by, his worry intensified, convincing him that the killer had really been after him, not Zagan. To take his mind off the brutal mutilation and death of his vicar general and off the killer who might return for him, he decided to take his yacht out for a spin. Now that Yo-Lin and her friends had given him the check for fifty thousand dollars he would be able to refurbish his 40 foot Apreamare 12.

Renato always seemed please to join him on the yacht. So he had Josette fix them a basket of food for their evening meal, and the two of them boarded the craft. Cruising down the river had always been an enjoyable experience. He loved the feel of the

480 horse power engine throbbing under his control, as he mastered the yacht through the center of the city and out into the countryside. What a relief it was to get away from Rosanada. They followed the river down to where it flowed into Lake Willandra. The open waters of the lake gave him a feeling of freedom, as he threw constraint to the wind and made the craft fly as fast as it could over the unruffled surface.

"Tomorrow will be a new day for us, Renato. I am making you my vicar general as well as my secretary. I am confident that you will live up to my expectations and do an admirable job."

"I will try my best, Excellency."

"We need to talk about some things I have had on my mind." L'Abbadon pushed his sailor cap back off his face and rubbed his prominent nose.

"Of course, what's on your mind?

"I like that young priest Malleus Shamrock. Someone recently made an allegation that he had abused him a couple years back, but then suddenly dropped the accusation."

"Yes, I recall that incident. What do you wish to do about it?"

"I want to send him to Saints Bacchus and Sergius Institute in New Orleans for psychological evaluation. If he is clean, then I will feel comfortable in reassigning him to parish duties. Will you arrange that for me? Call Shamrock and make an appointment to see him and set it up."

"But isn't it against canon law to do a psychological evaluation on a priest against his will?"

"How many times do I have to tell you that I make the rules in Rosanada. He goes to St. Bacchus." L'Abbadon cleared his throat and shook his finger at Renato as he spoke. Fire blazed in his eyes.

"I also want reports on Pompeo Dell'Anitra, Minimo Tabron, Marco Lamadrid, and all other priests who have been put on administrative leave. I also want a report on that priest who keeps complaining that his pastor has a gay lover that comes to his rectory occasionally on weekends and wants him to stay in a hotel for the time he is there."

"Consider it done, Excellency."

"One more thing, Renato. How many of our priests do you think have HIV and how many have full blown AIDS?

"That is impossible to determine, but I know at least 15 with AIDS and I would guess maybe another 15 with HIV."

"I really think we need to set up an AIDS seminar for all the clergy of the archdiocese and have attendance be compulsory. Take care of that too, Renato."

L'Abbadon reached over and patted Renato on the hand to soften the vehemence he had shown when Renato cited the canon law to prevent psychological evaluations of priests. He also knew how ambitious the man was and how eager he was to take over Zagan's position. "Well, all things do work together for the best," he mused.

"Now that Zagan is gone, I will have a vicar general who will be able to execute my commands, instead of a lush who is only interested in booze and catering to his personal comfort."

The cruise did lift his spirits. Zagan was gone and he and Renato would start working together to forge ahead. Zagan had been a dead weight and never did his share of the work. Although Renato was small of stature, had delicate features, and soft effeminate hands with long tapering fingers that were always pushing his heavy frame glasses up on his nose, he was a work horse.

When they arrived back at the archiepiscopal residence and tied the yacht up at the dock, L'Abbadon was in good humor and so was his vicar general. However, all that suddenly ended when they reached the backdoor of the house.

The security system had been breached. Josette always armed it when she left at the end of the day. Yet, someone had managed to open the door, turn off the system, and enter his private world. Perhaps, he reasoned, they might still be inside, waiting for him to return so they could murder him.

5
Renato

Renato could not help noticing how nervous L'Abbadon was. In response to his insistence that Brinks come immediately and reprogram the security system at the archiepiscopal mansion with a new keypad number and password, Renato called them and demanded instant attention. He himself did not like the idea of sleeping in a large house that had many hiding places for intruders. Even though the new system was in place by bedtime, he locked his bedroom door, pushed a heavy piece of furniture against it, and closed the shutters that decorated the windows, but also were functional.

Before he fell asleep, L'Abaddon knocked on his door, saying he had something to give him. Cautiously, Renato opened the door and the archbishop, dressed in lavender silk pajamas, entered His room and handed him a nine millimeter Beretta.

"Here Renato, put this under your pillow. And don't hesitate to use it," L'Abbadon commanded imperiously.

Cautiously Renato accepted the hand gun. "Thank you. Perhaps you could show me how to use it. I have never been one to use guns. I don't know the first thing about them."

"It is quite simple. It is semi-automatic. You just aim and shoot. There is really nothing to it," L'Abbadon said as he demonstrated the use of the gun and handed him an extra cartridge containing fifteen rounds.

Renato was seeing a side of the archbishop that he never even suspected existed. "Don't you want to keep it for your own protection, Your Excellency?"

"I have another one just like it. I sleep with it under my pillow. I don't intend to end up dead like Zagan. If you need to shoot, shoot to kill." With that remark the archbishop retired to his room for the night, after bolting the door behind him. Renato could hear him closing the shutters of the windows in his room also.

At daybreak, Renato was awakened by disturbing and unaccustomed noise coming from in front of the archiepiscopal residence. Throwing open the shutters, he looked out onto Coziness Lane where the yard in front of the house was filled with TV cameras and microphones. Reporters were crawling all over the place, barking orders to their television crews. He spotted a van bearing the CNN logo. CBS, FOX, MSNBC all had trucks lined up along the street as their crews were busy setting up equipment. Stunned, he realized they were going to hold a complete media circus right there in front of the mansion.

Picking up the morning *Rosanada News* that Josette had sent up to him on a breakfast tray in the dumb waiter that was installed conveniently with one in each bedroom of the house, he read the lurid headlines, telling of the murder of the vicar general. In the column that followed, every shocking detail was described explaining how the body had been mutilated.

VG Jan Zagan Murdered

Msgr. Jan Zagan, Vicar General of the Rosanada Archdiocese, was found dead in the swimming pool at the archbishop's residence at seven Coziness Lane in the Champs de Bauchery section of Rosanada. Wearing water wings, since he could not swim, he was found floating in four feet of water about nine yesterday morning by Msgr. Renato Del'Ano, secretary to Archbishop Cecil Anselm L'Abbadon. Zagan was completely naked, his shorts having been ripped from his body and tossed onto the side of the pool. The cause of death has been given as loss of blood and drowning. His penis was crudely chopped off and stuck into his mouth. The police have no clue as to why anyone would want to kill the vicar general. Homicide has started an investigation, because Zagan was obviously

a victim of foul play. Funeral services will
be held on Friday. Mass will be at eleven in
St. Mark's Cathedral with Archbishop
L'Abbadon officiating and interment will
follow immediately in one of the crypts on
the lower level of the church.

"Whew!" he thought, "wait 'til the nuncio hears
about this! He will notify the Prefect of the Clergy,
and soon Rome will be all over us." Very difficult
times lay ahead. Just how difficult, he never
imagined. He had personally invited all the American
cardinals and many bishops to attend the funeral for
Zagan that was to take place in two more days. Later
that very day the nuncio was due to arrive and they
would put him up in the room Zagan had used prior
to his death.

The papal nuncio, His Excellency Bishop
Roberto Cosimo Martino, a swarthy Italian, with a
heavy accent when he spoke English, arrived in time
for dinner. Renato had a limo sent to the airport to
pick him up. Since there was not room at the
mansion on Coziness Lane for all the cardinals and
bishops who were arriving for the Mass of
Resurrection for the dead Zagan, Renato rented the
entire top floor of the Hyatt Regency overlooking
the Rosanada River in the downtown section of the
city. He personally was there to welcome them when
they arrived. None of them were yet aware of the
full story of Zagan's murder and mutilation.

Cardinal John Frederick Watson of Dallas/Houston was the first to arrive, followed by Cardinal Henri François Jourdain of New Orleans/ Baton Rouge, and Cardinal Benjamin George Harris of Seattle. The bishops arrived in droves and Renato managed to see that they were all comfortably settled in their rooms and given carte blanche in the hotel restaurant. As the hierarchy continued to arrive, word began to spread among them of the ghastly details of Zagan's death. When they learned the unsavory details, they no longer wondered why L'Abbadon was not on hand to greet them when they arrived. Nevertheless, the bad news of Zagan's demise did not seem to put a damper on their conviviality, for they were renewing old friendships with colleagues they only saw on rare occasions such as funerals. Wine flowed freely and so did the conversation at the dinner Renato had arranged for them in the grand ballroom of the hotel.

Later that evening as Jan Zagan lay solemnly in state before the high altar of St. Mark's cathedral, L'Abbadon was present as all the members of the hierarchy filed by the body of the vicar general to pay their respects, greeting each one personally and receiving their condolences.

Renato had arranged everything for the Mass at the cathedral for Friday morning at eleven. L'Abbadon always loved a show and Renato knew that he was going to take full advantage of having his cathedral filled with notable members of the hierarchy to put on his very best performance.

Friday morning dawned and still the nuncio had not questioned them about Zagan's death. Perhaps he was waiting until after the interment.

That morning at breakfast Nuncio Martino was very circumspect and talked only about non controversial topics.

As usual, L'Abbadon asked Renato to lay out his clothing and help him dress. He insisted upon wearing one of his best Italian suits that a tailor in Rome made for him. Amazingly, he no longer appeared nervous, but rather seemed to thrive on the excitement of having so many of the hierarchy present in his cathedral to watch him officiate. The shot of diazepam that Renato injected into his vein before they left for the Mass of the Resurrection calmed him, until they arrived at the cathedral where the plaza in front of the old church was seething with mobs of people carrying placards protesting against the archdiocese.

Renato could hardly believe what he saw. As they made their way through the crowd with the help of two motorcycle cops and were close enough, he could read their signs and hear their chants. As their limo approached, the mobs closed in on them and chanted louder and louder while shaking their fists at them. "No more gay priests! "No more gay priests!" Others were yelling no more parish closings! "Keep our churches open!" A middle-aged man with a bullhorn was shouting, "Get rid of gay priests! No more lavender rectories! Down with liberal theologians who have no faith!" Still others were carrying signs and protesting the liberal take over of Catholic colleges that no longer taught true doctrine.

A milling throng blocked the entrance to the cathedral. CNN, FOX, MSNBC were filming the protest and the arrival of the various members of the hierarchy. Renato even caught a glimpse of Wayne Creasy, star reporter for the *Rosanada News* in the mob, eagerly photographing the protest.

Dumbfounded, Nuncio Martino merely stared at L'Abbadon in frigid silence. With difficulty, but with the help of the cops on motorcycles who by then had their sirens on full blast, Renato drove the archbishop's black limo through the protestors who, upon recognizing that the archbishop was arriving, began pelting the limo with tomatoes and eggs.

Quickly Renato jumped from the car, turning it over to a parking valet, and the three of them made their way toward the entrance of the old stone cathedral. Fortunately, Renato had requested that Mayor Kenneth Rafferty provide some of Rosanada's police force to meet L'Abbadon when they descended from the limo. Nevertheless the angry mob of protesters managed to pelt L'Abbadon with an egg that smashed on his forehead with its contents running down his face and dropping down onto his Italian silk suit, making an ugly yellow stain on his lapel, before he could make it safely inside.

The nuncio's icy demeanor stunned L'Abbadon

who was furious. "Why do they hate me so much?" he whispered to Renato, as he hastened to the sacristy to clean the egg from his face and clothing and remove his jeweled miter from the safe. In an attempt to put the situation in the best possible light, he said to the nuncio by way of explanation, "They are just pre Vatican II conservatives who can't keep up with the times." The nuncio just stared at him in a penetrating silence, which signified to Renato that they were in deep trouble. Renato could not have possibly imagined how serious a situation he faced.

6

Pompeo

It was hard to believe that Jan Zagan was dead and they were going to bury him that very day. A lot of changes were taking place at the chancery, not that it mattered much to him. Since he had been removed from his parish, St. Giordano Bruno, and given the assignment as chaplain at St. Francis Hospital and confessor to the nuns, the Sisters of St. Matrona, he had only one interest in life—trying to establish that he was not guilty of the allegations made against him by men who all had criminal records and were known to be active gay rights promoters. L'Abbadon refused to listen to him and, in fact, even refused to see him. Now that Renato Del'Ano had replaced Zagan as vicar general, he knew that he could expect no help from the chancery in defending his innocence. Although he detested living at Casa St. Popola, the house set up by L'Abbadon to house some of his prelates and pedophile priests, he could not afford to live elsewhere on what the archdiocese was giving him. The members of the hierarchy who lived at St. Popola were given spacious suites and private baths, but he had only a small room and had to share the bath with all the people that lived on his floor.

The *Rosanada Weekly Crier*, the archdiocesan newspaper, had just carried a notice that very morning that L'Abbadon had decided to elevate Reverend John N. Bugumil, J.C.D. to the episcopacy and that his consecration would be held shortly, the exact date to be announced later. Father Pompeo Dell'Anitra did not know the man, but Minimo Tabron, a priest friend who was due any minute to pick him up, could probably give him a complete rundown as they drove to the cathedral for the Mass of the Resurrection for Zagan. All that Pompeo knew was that Bugumil had been secretary to L'Abbadon prior to Renato Del'Ano.

No doubt he would get to know him better, because he would probably be moving into Zagan's suite at St. Popola's as soon as Zagan's things were removed, once the homicide squad finished their investigation. He had heard a lot of gossip about Bugumil.

Minimo Tabron proved eager to talk about the new bishop-elect as he pulled up in front of St. Popola's, where Pompeo was waiting for him on the porch. Immediately Pompeo noticed that Minimo had a young man with him. He never traveled alone, but made it his practice to serve as mentor to a young male. Once he had been arrested in Amsterdam for living with a minor Austrian boy without parental consent, and consequently deported to the United States. He had originally gone to Rome to study at the seminary, managed to get ordained, but lost his faith and spent time in a mental ward for schizophrenia. Then he had worked as a "male maid" in a Dutch brothel where all the girls were dressed up to look like pussy cats with very brief body suits that were cut high, exposing two inches of flesh above each thigh and wearing seductive black mesh stockings. To make them look like cats, they had large black velvet catlike ears fastened to their heads and long black velvet tails fastened to each of their bottoms that they swished around, as they flirted with their customers trying to attract them into their private cubicles. Minimo was dressed like a Tomcat—the same tight body suit as the girls, and a long black tail and huge black velvet ears fastened to his head. His costume did not include the mesh hose, so his hairy legs and knobby knees made his appearance utterly ludicrous. Since it was the only job he could get, he remained at it until he was deported by the police. After he returned to Rosanada, he resumed his standing in the archdiocese, because no one there knew of his checkered life in Europe.

Pompeo was always very careful to make no mention to Minimo of his erratic life in Amsterdam. Presently, since Minimo had been removed from his parish because of sexual allegation having been made against him, he was assigned as chaplain to a nursing home for the elderly at 13 Oblivion Lane in the very center of Daftmarsh, a withering little town near Rosanada. Jan Zagan said he should be thankful for that assignment, since allegations of sexual abuse had been made against him, and he could have given him no assignment at all.

As soon as Pompeo was seated in the backseat of Minimo's ten year old Ford, Minimo introduced his new protégé.

"Pompeo, meet Gautier d' Arras. He is from Port au Prince. Gautier, this is my old friend Pompeo Dell'Anitra."

Pompeo extended his hand over the shoulder of Gautier who was seated in the front next to Minimo. When their hands touched, somehow Gautier did not seem clean to him, and Pompeo felt like washing his hands to remove the taint of any pollution.

Pompeo could not help but notice the scars on the side of Gautier's face. One especially deep scar reached from the corner of his left eye down to his thick purplish black lips. Minimo had picked up some strange people in the past, but Gautier was the strangest of them all. His hair was plaited in little two inch long pigtails that stuck out all over his head. In his ears, he was wearing bulky gold earrings that dangled freely when he talked. What Pompeo found to be the strangest of all was the wild look that his eyes displayed from time to time.

"Too bad about the old man that was killed," Gautier said with a Haitian accent that betrayed his patois.

Because they did not acknowledge his comment, Gautier, determined to be noticed and deemed important continued, "My sister Josette knew him. She works for the archbishop in his house." Pompeo noticed that Gautier seemed to be proud to be in some way associated with the archbishop, but Minimo simply ignored his comments.

"Not to change the subject, but, Minimo, what can you tell, me about the Reverend John Bugumil?" Pompeo asked at they sped down the river road towards the center of the city. Just then they hit a pothole in the street and the car lurched. Minimo, who had always been clumsy, was not a very good driver.

"Sure, I can tell you all about him," replied Minimo, as he pulled down the sun visor to keep the glare of the morning sun out of his eyes. "I have seen him at Frankie's Gay Bar down on South Street. He is often there with Monsignor Paul F.X. Linde, the promoter of justice, and Monsignor Finolli, the director of vocations, who used to be secretary to Bishop Lingam and then was promoted to working permanently in the chancery at various jobs. Bugumil was secretary to the Queen for a short period of time, before being assigned to St. Sergius up the river."

Pompeo nodded knowing that Minimo always referred to L'Abbadon as the "Queen of the Cage aux Folles." Pompeo waited for Minimo to give him all the savory details. He was not disappointed, for

Minimo loved to talk and it was almost impossible to silence him once he got interested in a subject.

"He is known as Vlad, the Impaler, according to clerical gossip. He is a friendly enough guy with a big smile and a JCD degree. The Queen will probably make him judicial vicar."

When they arrived at the cathedral, a media circus was in full motion. CNN, FOX, and MSNBC were taping the loud demonstrators who were protesting the arrival of the archbishop and his entourage for the Mass with chants of "No more gay priests!" and "No more parish closings!"

Pompeo could see L'Abbadon making his way through the crowd with a couple policemen at either side while holding his head high, trying to ignore the seething protestors. Right behind him, Pompeo observed the papal nuncio and Monsignor Renato Del'Ano.

"Look," yelled Minimo, laughing loudly. "Someone just smashed a raw egg on L'Abbadon's head! Good show!" he exclaimed.

As Gautier went to park the car, Pompeo and Minimo pushed their way through the throng of protestors and into the cathedral where they took seats right on the center isle so that L'Abbadon would be sure to see that they were present.

After the archbishop vested in his finest regalia and began processing down the center aisle behind the cardinals, the nuncio, and various dignitaries of the Rosanada chancery, he looked about eight feet tall, for wearing his jeweled miter that was studded with genuine emeralds and rubies added considerably to his stature. His white vestments were embroidered in gold and were made of the finest silk. Arrogantly with head held high and his prominent nose leading the way, L'Abbadon seemed to glide through the nave, as the organ resounded to strains of *Ecce Sacerdos Magnus*. It was a classic performance in the best Catholic liturgical tradition.

"Look," Minimo exclaimed while nudging Pompeo. "He is wearing purple shoes and socks?"

"You mean, buskins, not shoes," Pompeo corrected with a superior lift of his eyebrows. "Archbishops wear buskins." Minimo, Pompeo reflected, always had more brawn than brains.

At this moment L'Abbadon was passing right beside him and Pompeo was sure that their presence had been observed.

All the concelebrants—the papal nuncio, the cardinals, and archbishops and various bishops from around the United States—took their places in the sanctuary. With great solemnity L'Abbadon began the liturgy. Pompeo was glad that it was not the nuncio who was celebrating the Mass, because he simply could not stand the way the Italian massacred the English language. He also hoped that he would not preach the homily and was relieved when L'Abbadon walked to the ambo, puckered his lips in his usual grimace and then launched into fulsome praise of Zagan, all but canonizing the murdered man.

At the conclusion of the Mass, pall bearers— priests of the archdiocese and favorites of L'Abbadon—carried the mortal remains of Jan Zagan from where it rested before the main altar and began a solemn procession down into the dark and winding crypts that lay in the subterranean reaches of the old cathedral. A place had been prepared for Zagan and was waiting to receive him. He would be interred in the floor in a side chapel where the light of day never reached. There were few to mourn for him and there would be fewer visitors to his grave—just a handful of curiosity seekers and the members of the press, of course.

Since there was so little room in the crypt, the only people to accompany Jan Zagan on his final trip were members of the hierarchy and of the Rosanada chancery. Pompeo, glad to escape with Minimo and Gautier who had rejoined them, whispered an Our Father for the repose of Zagan's soul and thought, "The old buzzard got just what he deserved!"

7
Forte

Two weeks dragged by and still he did not have a real lead in the case of the murder of Jan Zagan. The interrogation of L'Abbadon had provided Forte with no new information. A very taciturn archbishop relied on Puck, his attorney, to guide him through the questioning. He simply repeated what was already known. He had retired at eleven after saying good night to Zagan who went to the Olympic size pool behind the mansion. The next day he was found dead by Monsignor Renato Del'Ano.

In hope of getting some insight into the case, Forte had talked to some of the others at the chancery. Monsignor Finolli, the director of vocations, had been part of the chancery staff since before Zagan became vicar general. He had fine well-chiseled features, was about fifty, tall and slender with a mysterious and sophisticated appearance, but he seemed to be the perfect clergyman with his well-tailored black suit and tall Roman collar.

"Zagan was bound to have enemies," Finolli stated flatly. "A vicar general often has to make decisions that impact on others in ways they find objectionable. A lot of parishes have been closed. Last year we closed about ten. Some of the pastors were irate. I can't tell you much about that, you will have to ask Monsignor Stalker, the chancellor. He could brief you on that. That is about all I can think of to tell you, Forte."

Monsignor James Stalker, the chancellor and the former pastor of St. Mary Tudor's, one of the largest and most prestigious parishes of the archdiocese, was next on his list. A tall man, in his early seventies, and very distinguished, Stalker was busy at work in L'Abbadon's office, helping the archbishop with some particular matters, when Forte caught up with him. By then L'Abbadon had already left for the afternoon.

"Mind if I ask you a few questions, Chancellor?"

"Not at all, but there is really nothing I can tell you about Jan's death."

"I realize that, Monsignor. I know you were not at the scene of the crime. I just wanted to ask you what you could tell me about Zagan." Forte took the seat Stalker offered him just opposite him as he sat at L'Abbadon's black mahogany desk, puffing away at a cigar. Pulling a box of Thompson *Finas Dominicanas* from the bottom drawer of the desk, he offered Forte one.

Although he was not a cigar smoker, Forte relished the thought of smoking a really fine cigar and took one. Stalker picked up an unusual object

47

off the desk and handed it to him. It was about twelve inches tall and looked like the figure of a monk, complete in all details —a braided cord at the waist from which hung a rosary, a cowl draped in the back the way the Capuchins' wear theirs, a small breviary in one hand. Two diminutive blue stones looked up at him from the eyes of the heavy brass figurine.

"Interesting," commented Forte who was not sure why Stalker was showing him the statue.

"It is a lighter. Click that little wheel on his back and he will light your cigar for you," Stalker, an affable fellow, explained, with a twinkle in his eye.

Forte spun the wheel and a flame shot from the figure's mouth and lit his cigar. Since the lighter was quite heavy, he returned it to Stalker who placed it proudly on the archbishop's desk. "I gave it to him for his birthday last year," Stalker said as the two of them became engulfed in clouds of smoke.

Forte, anxious to get down to business, tried to draw the chancellor out by asking, "How long had you known Zagan?"

"I did not know him well. Let's see. Perhaps ten years, But we were never what you would call friends. I worked with him in the chancery; that was the extent of my relationship with him." Stalker had the habit of tugging on his chin when he was thinking.

"Did he have any enemies?"

"None that I know of."

"I understand that you have had to close quite a few parishes, is that right?" Forte asked with a penetrating glance. "You understand that I am asking you these questions so that we can protect all of you. We are of the opinion that Zagan was not the killer's real target. He might come back and strike again. I would appreciate anything you can tell me that will help further our investigation."

"I understand and appreciate your help and protection. Yes, to answer your question. We have closed many parishes because they could not pay their own way. We had no choice but to shut them down.

"Did that cause any trouble?"

"Nothing we could not handle. Some of the parishioners were outraged because their immigrant parents had built the parish."

"How about the pastors?"

"Well, as I recall, Father William J. King was irate when we closed St. Colon's. He was due to retire in four years and resented it bitterly that we closed his parish. About three months ago, he came blustering in here, yelling at the top of his lungs, that he had been treated unjustly."

"Where is he now? Forte made a mental note to visit Father King.

"He is at St. Cassiel's at 55 Curmudgeon Lane in the northwest of the city. It is a much smaller parish than the one he had and the rectory is much more modest than St. Cassiel's, which he had completely remodeled to his exact wishes and comfort." Stalker leaned back in his chair and puffed contentedly on his cigar. "It worked out well. He replaced a priest that we put on administrative leave because someone made very credible allegations of sexual abuse against him." Rising to his feet, he added. "We are taking care of him. Everything is working out."

"Anything else?"

"Well, we have had some problems with embezzlement in some parishes. Father King was involved in that too. I suggest you talk to the treasurer of the archdiocese about that. He would be the man to fill you in."

Realizing that he had obtained all the information he could from Stalker, Forte excused himself, thanked Stalker for the cigar, and then went to interview Bishop Morales, a man of about sixty, who had an office next to Renato Del'Ano's, and who was a soft spoken man with no comment. Then he stopped by the office of the bishop-elect, John Bugumil, who was busy unpacking his things and moving into the office recently vacated by Monsignor Del'Ano who had taken over Zagan's old office.

Bugumil struck Forte as being a very outgoing and jovial fellow who would make a good bishop. The soft gentle features of his face and his bright hazel eyes and warm smile seemed to welcome Forte, but at the same time his eyes were cold and calculating, as Forte introduced himself and began questioning him.

"There is really nothing I can tell you, Detective Forte," he said with the aplomb of a Washington diplomat. I am just moving into the chancery today, as you can see.

He handed Bugumil his card. "If you think of anything that might help us solve this crime, call me."

He had one more person he wanted to interview before quitting for the day—Father Minimo Tabron, who had been removed from his pastorate and sent as chaplain to a home for the elderly in Daftmarsh.

Father Tabron actually welcomed his visit and was eager to talk. He answered all his questions in such detail that Forte found it necessary at times to interrupt him and change the subject in order to go on with his next question. He had no idea of who might want to murder Zagan or anyone else. All in all, Tabron seemed harmless enough, but Forte surmised that he, in fact, was gay.

The whole day was a bust. Completely discouraged, Forte headed for home. As he drove his white Impala through the city traffic, he kept remembering his visit with Miguel, his son, the day before. They had had a wonderful time together assembling a model ship that he had bought at the toy shop in the Rosanada Mall. The two of them worked on it all weekend long. It was really wrenching when Anita came for the boy Sunday night to take him away.

"Please mom," Miguel begged. "Can't you stay here? Can't we be with Dad?" Forte knew what his son was going through, because many of his friends had divorced and he had seen what it had done to their children.

Anita turned a deaf ear to her son's pleas. "It is time to go home now, Miguel. Pack up your things. At once!" She just stood there in the living room, glaring at Forte, with her face contorted by a pout.

Why his petite and pretty wife had broken up their home was something Cristian Forte could not understand. He didn't drink—excessively that is. He was never unfaithful—always treated her with respect. Maybe he was a bit macho sometimes. Perhaps he insisted too much on having his own way.

Her dark amber eyes avoided his, as their son pleaded to stay in the lovely little Cape Cod home he had provided for them. It was modest, but he was a good provider. They never lacked for anything. As a homicide detective he made good money. Of course, she did complain that he had to work a lot at night when he was in hot pursuit of a killer, but that was unavoidable.

How much he wanted to take Anita in his arms and hold her tight and cover her protests with kisses, but she quickly grabbed Miguel by the arm and dragged the protesting boy to the car.

The house was utterly empty when they were gone. He proceeded to put away the glue and the paints that he and Miguel had used to make their ship. "O God," he prayed. "I can't live alone."

Depression settled in upon him. Why couldn't he get a handle on the Zagan murder? Mentally he made a list of people he wanted to contact— Father King and of course the priests whose names were on the list Stalker's secretary had given him—Bocchino Martinelli, Clitor S. Del Sapo, Marco Lamadrid, Minimo Tabron, Pompeo Dell'Anitra, Camino Velvet, and about ten others. He would also have to arrange a talk with Yo-Lin Sin. Perhaps she might give him the lead he was looking for. Yes, he would have to contact the woman known as the Queen of Sex and Drugs.

8

Renato

As he waited for L'Abbadon to leave for the chancery, Renato stood staring into the waters of the indoor pool that separated the living salon from the dining room in the archiepiscopal mansion. Every morning it was the same story. The archbishop dawdled at breakfast and was never in a hurry to go to the chancery. He never scheduled more than one appointment in the morning and only one in the afternoon.

The drive to the office was uneventful, and Renato had a lot on his mind. A lot had happened. Now that he was vicar general, his hands were really full, and although he needed to get to the office earlier, L'Abbadon was never ready before 9:30.

When they parked behind the chancery, L'Abbadon handed him his briefcase and expected him to carry it for him. Together they took the elevator that lead to the third floor to their suite of executive offices overlooking the Rosanada River. Renato waited while the archbishop fished in his pants' pocket for the keys to his office. When he had found them he handed them to Renato. "Here open the door for me," he ordered, expecting Renato to jump to his every wish.

He took the keys and selecting one, inserted it in the lock and threw open the door. Unprepared for what he saw, he staggered at the sight of Chancellor James Stalker sprawled on the floor before L'Abbadon's desk in a pool of blood with a large bloody gash on his right temple. On his forehead, painted in his own blood was an inverted pentagram! The archbishop's heavy cigar lighter, obviously the murder weapon, lay beside him.

When L'Abbadon saw the dead chancellor, he let out a loud banshee wail and collapsed in the chair behind his desk. Renato knew that the first thing he had to do was calm the archbishop to get him ready for what lay ahead. He reached into the top drawer of L'Abbadon's desk and pulled out a syringe and a bottle of diazepam and injected him with it. Then he poured him a full glass of Scotch and watched as L'Abbadon downed it in one gulp.

Quickly he punched the numbers 911 into his cell phone and asked for homicide. He also called Puck and expected the attorney for the archdiocese to come immediately for the interrogation that would follow.

The vicar general and the chancellor had both been murdered. Would he, the new vicar general, be next? Not if he could help it! He patted the pistol in his jacket pocket, and felt certain that L'Abbadon was also armed. Nevertheless, the archbishop was very nervous with every sound making him jumpy.

"Good morning, gentlemen," Forte greeted them as he and Attorney Puck arrived at the same time. "Please, all of you be seated in the conference alcove over there on the other side of the room." He pointed to the long mahogany table, surrounded by matching chairs that lay alongside the windows opposite the archbishop's desk. After taking a look at Stalker's bloody corpse, he directed his crew to begin their operations.

"Has anything been moved, Archbishop L'Abbadon, since you entered the room and discovered the body?" Forte motioned for his men to photograph the scene. As the flash bulbs popped, Renato watched L'Abbadon shield his eyes and knew that the archbishop was having another one of his migraines.

"No, nothing has been moved." L'Abbadon replied emphatically. "Look, Detective, someone tried to kill me last night. I demand police protection twenty-four/seven. I want a squad car observing my residence at all times." L'Abbadon was adamant and rose to his feet and walked towards Forte taking an aggressive stance. "My life is in danger. What are you going to do about it?"

"Please sit down, Your Excellency, all in due time. First, I need to ask you some questions." He glanced at Puck and waited for the attorney to signal his consent.

"Where were you last night, Your Excellency?"

"I was here in my office working with Stalker from about eight until ten. Monsignor Del'Ano brought me here, dropped me off, and returned to pick me up at ten."

"You can verify that, Monsignor Del'Ano?" Forte walked over to where he was standing, and Renato replied. "Yes, that is true."

"Did you see Stalker when you picked him up?"

"No, I did not. I parked the limo at the entrance to the chancery and waited for Archbishop L'Abbadon to come out."

"And you, Archbishop, was everything in order when you left Stalker? Nothing seemed out of the ordinary?"

"Everything was fine," L'Abbadon replied laconically. "We were working on some parish closings. Checking records. When I left, Jim said he was going to work a little later than I, and that he hoped to finish about midnight."

"Did you lock the door of your office when you left?"

"Yes, and the main entrance door was locked downstairs. We always keep it locked at night."

The homicide squad was just finishing its work investigating the scene and was in the process of zipping Stalker's body up in a body bag. As Forte continued asking questions, they wheeled the corpse away on a gurney.

"The door was locked when you both arrived this morning?"

Forte looked intently first at l'Abbadon and then at Renato.

"I myself unlocked it, Detective."

"Does anyone else have a key to your office, Archbishop?" Forte asked.

"No one."

Forte examined the door and its lock, observing what Renato already knew. The door locked automatically when you closed it, if it was programmed to do so."

Renato could see the wheels turning in Forte's mind. Whoever killed Stalker must have had a key or was someone he knew well and admitted into his office. Obviously the detective found it most unusual that the vicar general had been killed at the archiepiscopal mansion and the chancellor in L'Abbadon's office to which only the archbishop had a key.

"I want a list of any and all priests who have experienced any kind of disciplinary action in the past five years, including those whose parishes have been permanently closed, and the ones I read about in the *Rosanada News* last summer who were caught embezzling funds from the Church. For your own protection, Monsignor Renato and Archbishop L'Abbadon, I am requesting this information. A brutal killer has struck members of this chancery. He might strike again. You must be very careful, both of you."

"With the permission of our attorney, I will have

the secretary prepare the information for you." L'Abbadon glanced at Puck who nodded slightly.

"One final word, neither you, Your Excellency, or Monsignor Del'Anno is to leave town. Is that clear?"

It was perfectly clear. Renato now realized that Detective Forte had placed his name on his list of suspects along with that of the archbishop, since they both had been present at both crime scenes at the time of the murders.

Puck also took his leave, but not before telling them not to answer any questions at all without his being present.

Renato drove L'Abbadon to the mansion and left him locked in his bedroom with a bottle of Scotch, holding his poodle, Pigalle, on his lap, while Josette prepared his lunch and sent it up to him in the dumbwaiter.

Wishing that he were anywhere but Rosanada, Renato returned to the chancery and settled into Zagan's office. He did not have the luxury of lounging at home like L'Abbadon did. He had appointments to keep. The first was with Malleus Shamrock. Two years earlier a young fifteen year old male had accused Shamrock of molesting him. The youth had gone to his pastor and lodged a complaint against him. Then he actually came into the chancery and talked with Zagan about it. Renato checked in Zagan's secret files and found that he had never reported the incident to the police. The file indicated that he had moved Shamrock to Daftmarsh as parochial vicar of St. Dymphna's, where he was currently assigned. St. Dymphna's was a very small parish that had never been large, but had dwindled considerably in recent months.

"Please be seated, Father Shamrock." The young priest seemed nervous as he took the chair across the desk from Renato. A good looking Irishman in his early thirties, Shamrock had blue eyes, black hair, and a winning smile.

"Good day to you, Monsignor," he replied extending his hand in greeting.

"Well, there is no need for us to take up a lot of time," he said. "I will come right to the point. I am closing St. Dymphna's immediately." Renato waited to see what effect these words would have on Shamrock, who registered surprise.

"What is my new assignment, Monsignor?" he asked with a look of anticipation, knowing that almost any other assignment in the archdiocese would be better than the one he had.

"We are not giving you another assignment, Father Shamrock." Renato wanted to toy with him a while before announcing his plans for the young priest.

"I am afraid I don't understand." Bewilderment was written on Shamrock's handsome and regular black Irish features.

"Let me explain then. We have investigated this allegation of sexual abuse that Bob Reilly made against you and see that the young accuser has dropped his complaint. You have a good record." Renato laid the young priest's personnel file on the desk in front of him and flipped through it.

"I am totally innocent, Monsignor. Bob Reilly had no reason to accuse me," he said as he twisted uncomfortably in the black leather chair.

"His Excellency Archbishop L'Abbadon and I have come up with a solution. We are sending you to you Saints Bacchus and Sergius Institute in New Orleans for psychological evaluation." Renato watched as the young priest continued to squirm under his gaze.

"But," he protested, "that is against canon law which absolutely forbids psychologically evaluating priests against their will." Shamrock's lower lip trembled as he spoke and his face became flushed.

"I must remind you of your vow of obedience to His Excellency." To enforce his words, he rose to his feet and towered over Shamrock. "If you refuse to go, we will have no choice but to start a process to defrock you." Renato tapped his finger on the table for emphasis.

"How is that possible?" Shamrock stammered. A priest cannot be defrocked by administrative decision." Fear shone in his blue eyes.

"Of course, we would hold a canonical trial. Monsignor Linde, the promoter of justice, would take care of everything. You would be defrocked, I guarantee you. We simply cannot have our priests becoming sexually involved with youth."

Realizing that he had no choice in the matter, Shamrock slumped in the chair and sighing deeply, asked, "When do I go to New Orleans?"

"They are expecting you next Monday. I have made all the arrangements. You can get the details from Marianne on your way out. She will tell you everything you need to know." Renato walked around his desk and extended his hand to Shamrock terminating the interview.

As soon as Shamrock left, Renato asked Marianne to send a letter to Father Minimo Tabron, informing him that the archdiocese was closing St. Dymphna's and that he was to discontinue saying Mass there on the weekends.

He then met with Msgr. Harry Rattlet, the treasurer of the archdiocese, a very discrete womanizer, he had heard, and Msgr. Toccafondi, the financial advisor, and discussed the closing of several other parishes. St. Helen's, St. Joan of Arc, and St. Francis would all be closed before the end of the year. He directed that letters be sent to the pastors of these churches at once, notifying them of their immanent closure. The pastors would be reassigned to parishes where they had removed other pastors because credible sexual allegations had been made against them. Yes, thought Renato. Everything does work together for the best. However he was not too sure about what good would come from the death of Monsignor James

Stalker.

Because he wanted to get home to the mansion before dark, he left his office shortly before five. He couldn't be too careful under the circumstances. Buttoning up his topcoat and pulling his black felt hat down over his brow to make himself less obtrusive, he hurried out the door of the chancery to his Lexus.

When he arrived home, Josette was preparing dinner, and L'Abbadon was sitting in the drawing room holding his little poodle in his lap and sitting before his bigger than life portrait of himself in his formal attire, surrounded by burning candles that made it look like a shrine. He was brushing the poodle, adjusting her rhinestone collar, and tying a pink ribbon to her collar. Renato watched as L'Abbadon sprayed the poodle with Lolita Lempicka au Masculin Fraîcheur, his own brand of cologne.

"Good evening, Renato, pour me a drink of Scotch,"

Renato did as he was bidden. The poodle jumped from L'Abbadon's lap and came running to Renato and stood waiting for him to pick her up.

"Look out and tell me if you can see the police car that is protecting me," L'Abbadon commanded.

"I see it, Your Excellency."

Somehow Renato could not imagine that the police car in front of the mansion would be very much protection, if someone decided they wanted to commit murder. After eating a light dinner—he had no appetite —he retired early to his room and placed his Baretta under his pillow. If someone wanted to kill him, they would be in for a fight.

9
Minimo

With keys in hand, Minimo climbed up the warped boards of the steps at the entrance of St. Dympha's, thrust the key in the lock, and threw open the door of the poor little church. L'Abbadon had decided to close St. Dympha's permanently. It was absolutely the last straw! He had been accused of sexually molesting a man ten years ago when he was still a minor. A felon and a gay activist, the man had never proved his case against Minimo, but nevertheless, L'Abbadon paid him off, giving him seventy-five thousand dollars without his having to go to court or even swear out a deposition, simply because the archbishop was determined not to be cross-examined on the witness stand. He had hidden the sexual crimes of too many priests against minors and was not about to be convicted of aiding and abetting a felon.

A few months ago, the old bastard sent him a letter saying he was not fit to be a pastor and sent him to Daftmarsh to a home for the elderly where half of the people were suffering from dementia.

On weekends he had been helping Malleus

Shamrock, the parochial vicar at St. Dymphna's, saying the Saturday evening Mass. Now the last shred of his dignity had been taken from him, because L'Abbadon had decided to close St. Dymphna's permanently. The building was in disrepair—an old wooden structure with asphalt shingles for siding and a tin roof that leaked. Only about fifty people could assemble there at any given time. Cheap plaster statues, chipped and faded, grotesquely watched over the people as they came and went.

Minimo crossed through the small vestibule and pushed open the swinging doors that led into the church proper. His glance fell upon the bleeding statue of St. Sebastian that stood next to the holy water font. The saint must have had a hundred gaping wounds where the arrows of his executioners pierced his flesh, causing his martyrdom. It was a nice statue, but Minimo preferred the one of St. Dymphna in the sanctuary. She was holding her severed head with her left hand, placing it firmly on the bleeding stump of her neck. According to legend she was the daughter of a pagan Irish king who became Christian. When her mother died her father wanted to take her into his bed, causing her to flee with the priest Gerebernus to Belgium. Her father pursued them and unable to convince his daughter to go to bed with him, he killed the priest who was protecting her and struck off her head with a sword wielded by his own hands. The statue of Dymphna was especially grotesque because she had a chain in her right hand and fastened to it and lurking at her feet was a demon with black curling tail and fiery red eyes. Before the statue of the saint blazed row upon row of votive candles glowing red in their cheap glass holders. Some of them were sputtering and on the verge of going out.

He had come to St. Dymphna's to collect some of his things that he had left in the sacristy—a faded purple stole, a breviary, and a surplice. As he hurried out the center aisle in the darkened church, he heard someone come in the door that he had left unlocked when he entered. It was getting late in the day and the windows made of cheap red, blue and green glass permitted very little light to enter.

"Hi, Father Minimo."

It was Jamie Shannon, the eighteen year old son of a widow who worked long hours at the Rosanada paper mill to earn a living for herself, Jamie, and his fourteen year old brother Joey. Her husband had died the year before and she was having difficulty coping with the two boys who kept getting into trouble.

"Hello, Jamie. Good to see you. What's on your mind?"

"I saw you come in here, Father, and I was hoping we could talk." The boy dipped his finger in the holy water font and signed himself with the cross, before proceeding out of the church.

"Sure, Jamie, any time. The archbishop is closing

this church immediately, but we can still be friends, if you like. I would like to continue being your friend."

Eagerly the boy started down the front steps of the church and tripped on the warped boards and fell twisting his ankle. When he tried to stand on the injured ankle, he found he could not.

Muscular and strong in spite of his sixty years, Minimo pulled the boy to his feet and with the boy's arm around his sturdy shoulders helped him walk down the street to the Shannon home. When they arrived, the house was deserted.

Depositing the youth on the well-worn brown sofa in the living room, Minimo asked, "Where is your mother?"

"She's at the paper mill and won't be home until seven. She never gets home before then?"

"And your brother Joey?"

"Delivering papers. He has a pretty long route. He will be back about seven too."

"Your ankle is quite swollen. I'll massage it, but first let me get some ice in the kitchen to put on it."

The poverty of the Shannon family was very obvious. All the furniture was stained and coming apart at the seams. Plastic draperies decorated with floral arrangements hung at all the windows concealing the world outside. A small black and white television sporting rabbit ears was in the corner of the living room.

The kitchen appeared to be the room where the

family spent most of its time. There was a white porcelain-top table with chipped marks that revealed the base metal underneath. Chairs for Jamie, Joey, and their mother sat primly at the table. Across the room under the kitchen window was a fourth chair that their father had used before his early death. Fumbling in the refrigerator, Minimo found a tray of ice and dumped it in a plastic bag that he found in a box on the table.

Jamie was genuinely pleased that Father Minimo was taking the trouble to help him. "Gee, Father, it is really great of you to do this for me," he said pushing his curly blonde hair back from his handsome boyish face.

"You said you had something you wanted to talk to me about, Jamie?" Minimo smiled at him encouraging him to speak. Seeing that the ankle was too swollen for him to massage it, Minimo placed the ice bag on it. "You can tell me anything."

"Oh, yes." It is just that…" The boy hesitated.

"Go ahead, you can tell me."

"I want to be just like you when I grow up. I want to be a priest. Will you help me to do that?" The boys blue eyes probed his. Perhaps you could come over here after I get out of school in the afternoons and tell me what I have to learn?"

Minimo delighted in being mentor to young men, especially when they were as engaging as Jamie.

"Well, let's see. You are eighteen and will graduate from high school next June. There is a lot

69

I could teach you and maybe help you find a seminary for next Fall. Of course, we will be great friends. You just stay here until your mom comes home and can look after that ankle. I'll stop by here tomorrow after school to see how you are doing. Just keep the ice on it, until it stops hurting."

Saying goodbye to Jamie Shannon, Minimo rushed back to Happy Manor Home for the Elderly to be in time for dinner. When he arrived there, he found Gautier waiting for him.

The Haitian seemed to be bursting with something to tell him as they sat together in his room waiting for dinner to be served. Laughing and shaking his head so that his golden earrings dangled against his neck, he kicked off his shoes and leaned back in the overstuffed chair by the window. The room was small, causing Minimo to feel cramped. He was used to having a large rectory at his disposal, but now he had been reduced to living in a tiny room that didn't even have a TV. All he had was an iron bed, a small night stand beside it, a chest of drawers, and a mirror. There was one picture of a waterfall on the wall. He had removed the crucifix from the wall and tossed it in a dresser drawer "Well, tell me what's up?" Minimo prodded.

The Haitian scratched his head and brushed his pigtails back with the palm of his hand, jangling his gold earrings.

"Wait 'til you hear what Josette says."

"Josette?"

"You know, *ma soeur*. She works as maid for the archbishop in his big house." Gautier slapped his hand on his thigh and chuckled out loud.

"Your sister works in the archbishop's residence?"

"Yeah, I told you that the day we went to the cathedral together. She does, and she says the old man is a faggot. She says the man who died in the pool was also one. She says that Monsignor Del'Ano is one too! She says she has seen them horsing around."

"Well, I suspected that" Minimo replied. "It doesn't surprise me in the least. I recently read a book by an ex-priest called Kelly who says that a large number of priests in this country are gay and many of the bishops also are." He sighed deeply, scratched his head, and became silent. After a few moments he continued speaking. "Sure, I think Kelly is right. But there is no way they can get rid of all of us. However, it makes me mad as hell that he took my parish away for fooling around with a minor. I guess he is one of those people who believe that the most important commandment is 'Thou shall not get caught.' What else did Josette tell you?" Minimo searched the deep brown eyes of his protégé, eager to hear what he had to say.

"She says that they're scared. Plenty scared. Both of them L'Abbadon and Del'Ano. She says they both are packing pistols."

As soon as dinner was over and he had said the

71

night prayers over the mike for all the bedridden elderly, Minimo climbed into Gautier's old Plymouth and went to spend the night with his protégé in his apartment over Frankie's Bar. Since it was Friday night, there would be a big celebration at Frankie's. A lot of priests he knew would be there. They would make a night of it— he and Gautier. It would be a real blast. He smiled at the anticipated pleasure of the night ahead.

He was not disappointed. The Friday night crowd was larger than usual. Minimo spotted Monsignors Finolli and Linde, both of whom were regular visitors to Frankie's and made no attempt to hide their gay proclivities. Both were dressed casually in faded jeans and knit shirts that read "Gay and Proud of It." Previously at Frankie's, Minimo had even seen Finolli, who had an in-your-face attitude, and was known for marching in gay parades. If L'Abbadon knew anything about it, he closed a blind eye to it.

Because he, Minimo, had gotten involved with a minor, he was on L'Abbadon's black list. The old bastard even told him that he would never assign him as pastor to another parish. He felt as if he were going to explode. Life at Happy Manor Home for the Elderly was more than he could bear.

Gautier was good company for him. The young fellow was eighteen and no longer a minor and safe to be with. He wasn't about to get involved with any minors. Actually Gautier was the center of attention at Frankie's, because he brought his voodoo drums with him and in frenzy beat them to the music of a Calypso band. It amused Minimo that Gautier told him that he was a priest too—a voodoo priest.

"I'll show you sometime how I sacrifice a chicken," Gautier promised during an intermission of the music. The rum they were drinking had freed him from his inhibitions, and he began describing voodoo ritual to Minimo who was utterly entranced by what Gautier was telling him.

"Yeah," Minimo exclaimed gleefully. "I want to see that. I might show you a few things too." He also thought about Jamie Shannon and about what he and Gautier could do with him. "Just wait," he whispered in Gautier's ear. "Just wait till you see what I can do."

10

Marco Lamadrid

When Detective Forte arrived at Grace Pentecostal Chapel, Marco Lamadrid was busy taping his national telecasts for the Christian Network of America. CNA carried his program for thirty minutes, five mornings a week. It was all done by tapes that he made in his studio and sent to them. He was finally free from L'Abaddon who had driven him out of the priesthood. Now he could happily serve God as he had been called to do.

The Church had gone crazy with homosexuals in control at all levels. Cardinals, archbishops, priests, seminarians dedicated to the gay life had driven him and many others good priests from their parishes. To cover their own homosexual activity they made scapegoats of men like him who did not share their sexual orientation.

Just recently he read in the *Rosanada News* that a certain priest, one Father Patrick Flynn, was suing the archdiocese because the pastor he was assigned to work with received visits on the weekends from his homosexual lover. Protesting that he, as a non gay, was being discriminated against by the archbishop, he filed a lawsuit stating that the archbishop told him to take a room at the Holiday Inn when the pastor's lover came to the rectory. He could not bear the unholy activity that was taking place every weekend behind the closed doors of his pastor's suite of rooms.

As soon as Marco learned that the man who had knocked on his office door was a homicide detective, he invited him to take a seat and offered him a soft drink.

"What can I do for you, detective?" Marco ventured as he sipped his ginger ale. He would have preferred drinking a beer, but now that he had become Pentecostal, he was forced to give up his taste for anything alcoholic.

"I was hoping you could give me a few leads that I might follow in hopes of finding out who killed the vicar general and the chancellor." Forte could see that Lamadrid was utterly content with his new life. But you never could tell. He might still bear a grudge against the chancery officials who drove him out of the Church and be willing to talk.

"I really don't have any contact with them. I stay clear of all of them." He finished his drink and tossed the empty can in the trash basket beside his desk. "Some of my friends told me that Father Colin Olid, who is currently pastor at the Santiago Church, is blaming me for his failure to send in substantial amounts of money to the archdiocese, like I used to send them when I was there. He says the dwindling membership there is due to my making allegations against him. I just wish they would leave me in peace. I have had enough of their trying to make me a scapegoat for their failings. From what I hear, Olid is running me down to every one he can at the chancery. He is probably afraid that they will close down Santiago and send him to a less desirable assignment."

"Thanks, Reverend. I appreciate your help. I will check him out." Knowing that Lamadrid had no more to contribute, Forte said goodbye and left.

11

Forte

He was going around in circles. There was no end to the intricacies of the discontent in the archdiocese and the chancery. Someone obviously was disgruntled enough to kill and he had to find out who it was before they killed again. Perhaps a visit to Yo-Lin Sin was in order. He decided to visit her at *La Estrella d'Amor*, her nude bar in the mountains north of Rosanada.

When he entered Yo-Lin's she was busy working on her receipts and accounts in a small room behind the bar. He introduced himself and explained that he was the homicide detective on the chancery murders.

"I'd like to ask you a few questions. I will only take up a little of your time," he said extending his hand to her.

"Welcome, Detective Forte," she exuded her charms. "Let me have them bring you a drink. What would you like?" Her breasts, like melons, were peeking out over the top of a low cut Oriental tunic of red silk. When she crossed her legs, the tunic slid above her knees, and she smiled at him enticingly. He knew her type and decided at once that she was a nymphomaniac and no doubt came on at any man who approached her.

"I don't drink when I'm on duty. Give me Perrier water, please" He decided to play along with her. He winked at her flirtatiously and smiled.

"And why does your duty bring you here to see me? I am completely above board—legal in every way, I assure you. I'm completely legitimate now and have been for years." She drew her chair closer to his.

"I thought that perhaps you could help give me some clues and leads as to who is murdering the priests of the chancery. I understand that you are a good friend of the archbishop."

"Yes, Cecil and I are friends, but I have no idea who the murderer might be."

"Could it possibly be the Latino Mafia? The way that Zagan died suggests a Mafia assassination." She had drawn her chair so close to his that now she was in his face.

"No one in the Latino Mafia had any reason to kill Zagan. They liked him and contributed to the charities of the archdiocese quiet liberally. No, it wasn't the Mafia. I would have heard if any of them had it in for Zagan." She reached out and laid her slender hand with its green enameled nails on his arm and patted it affectionately. "Look, Detective, why don't you come back some night soon and see our nude review. I personally will make you very welcome. Here are a couple tickets for the show." She tucked the tickets in the pocket of his blazer.

Thanking her for her generosity, he left with absolutely no intention of returning for the review. In fact, he was angered that she would even suggest that he might be interested in such things.

Hoping that a visit to Father King would be helpful, Forte drove to 55 Curmudgeon Lane, where he found the pastor of St. Cassiel's opening parishioners Sunday envelopes and counting the money he removed from them. Forte had read in the newspaper some months back that King had been accused of embezzling $40,000. from St. Colon's where he had been pastor before the archdiocese closed his parish and sent him to St. Cassiel's. The archbishop had been able to get a good price for St. Colon's from a congregation of Baptists. He would no doubt use the money, Forte reasoned, to pay off the many men who were claiming sexual abuse, citing priests as offenders.

Father King, past seventy, walked with a cane. He was a heavy man, but still quite strong and vigorous, except for the limp he had when he walked, favoring his left leg. Turning his back on the little stacks of bills and checks on his desk, he growled at Forte: "What are you here for?"

"I'd like to ask you some questions. I am Detective Forte of homicide and I am investigating the murders of the vicar general and the chancellor of the archdiocese," he explained ignoring the gruffness of King's greeting.

"What do you mean coming here and questioning me. I don't know anything about what goes on in the chancery?' he growled.

Forte noticed that the priest's sport shirt bore yellow stains that he surmised were from his breakfast eggs. His black slacks were shiny at the knees and wrinkled.

"I heard you were pretty unhappy about the closing of St. Colon's and your transfer here." From the pastor's office he could see into a very middle-class living room furnished with a cheap floral covered sofa and two chairs to match. A small screen television was tuned to the news on the local channel where the anchor man was discussing the murders of the chancellor and the vicar general.

Father King got quiet and both men listened to what the news anchor was saying:

"The chancellor was killed by a blow to his right temple and forehead and had been dead about eleven hours when his body was discovered by Archbishop L'Abbadon and Monsignor Del' Ano. According to forensics, the killer must have had great strength to overpower the chancellor and bring him down with a blow from a curious heavy brass cigar lighter made to look like a monk. The most unusual thing about the murder is that the killer painted an inverted pentagram on the victim's forehead, suggesting perhaps a cult assassination.

The police, who have not yet made a break in the Zagan murder in over two weeks, are completely stymied. Our next newscast will be at five this afternoon."

"Well," said King gruffly, "I'm glad I don't work in the chancery. Dangerous business." His eyes were like small beads as they focused on Forte.

"You are due to retire in four years, aren't you?" he inquired of the old priest who seemed reluctant to discuss anything with him.

"Yep."

"They closed St. Colon's and moved you here a few months ago?"

"Yep."

"I read in the *Rosanada News* that the parish council at St. Colon's accused you of embezzling money. Is that true?"

"I have nothing to hide, Detective. I just borrowed a bit of money, Only forty thousand dollars. I needed to buy a new car. The one I had was worn out. I could have gone to the parish council and asked them for an advance. I planned to pay the money back. I am not a thief," he protested vigorously as the clock on the mantle in the living room struck two.

Deciding to let the priest talk as much as he would now that he had begun, Forte kept quiet.

"I am not a thief. Lots of pastors in Rosanada keep two bank accounts. They accumulate funds in bank accounts set up in the name of their parish. It is common practice. The archdiocese only lets a pastor keep a hundred thousand in the parish bank account. All other money is to be turned over to the archdiocese. Many pastors salt some away to have if emergencies arise. Bill Daley, the president of the parish council found my second account and reported me to the vicar general. That is all there was too it," he stated flatly, trying to exonerate himself from all blame.

"Where were you the night Zagan was killed? You realize, of course, that you don't have to answer that question without the presence of an attorney," he said trying to frighten King into believing that he was a suspect.

"I was right here in the rectory watching television."

"Can anyone verify that?"

"No," he said sullenly.

"And the night the chancellor was killed?"

"Same thing. I was here watching television. Look, Detective, I have some parish business I have to take care of now, if you are done with me?" King was beginning to sweat and obviously anxious for him to leave.

"That will be all for this afternoon, but do not leave town."

12

Jamie

St. Dymphna's was deserted. Jamie watched as Father Shamrock stripped the altar, emptied the tabernacle, and left the tabernacle door standing open. The sanctuary candle no longer burned, nor did the votives before the statue of St. Dymphna. He had removed the altar vessels and his vestments and packed them in his car. Before taking one last look around the church, he said goodbye to Jamie, and then rushed out to his car and disappeared out of sight down the street.

He would miss Father Shamrock whose altar boy he had been for the past two years. However, Father Minimo had been very nice to him, since he fell and twisted his ankle. He had stopped by to see him twice since then and had even obtained his mother's permission to take him to meet his friend from Haiti, Gautier. Father Minimo said that Gautier knew all kinds of neat tricks and would show him some.

Father Minimo seemed pleased that he wanted to become a priest like him. The last time he saw him,

Father Minimo said he had special plans for him. He did not say what they were, but Jamie was sure he was going to teach him things to help him get into a seminary and become a priest.

When Father Minimo stopped by to see him on Saturday, he had not been at home, because he and Joey had gone to visit their grandmother Lois. There was not much to do at her house, except shoot the basketball through a hoop with eighteen year old Miguel Forte who came on weekends to visit his father, a detective for the Rosanada police, who lived next door. Miguel came Friday nights to spend the weekend, but his father had to work Saturdays until four in the afternoon. For this reason Jamie's Grandmother Lois fixed lunch for the three boys in her warm and cozy kitchen. He felt sorry for the boy whose mother had moved out taking Miguel with her. They had seemed like a happy family until just a few months ago. In fact, Jamie had felt a bit envious of their family, since his own father had died and his mother was having such a difficult time to pay the bills.

Miguel actually seemed envious of him now, especially because he told him that he was going to become a priest.

"You mean a priest like Father Colin Olid at Santiago?" the boy asked wide-eyed.

"I don't know him," Jamie replied as he tossed a basketball for the boy to catch. "I am going to be a priest like Father Minimo. He is a great priest. In fact, he is going to give me lessons."

Jamie could see that Miguel was impressed. He was a month older than Miguel, a bit taller than he, and even had more whiskers on his chin. The day went by fast. Joey spent the morning watching cartoons on the television while he and Miguel shot hoops. Jamie fell asleep that night thinking about how Father Minimo was going to teach him so much that he needed to know, so he could become like him.

13

Forte

Although he kept interviewing suspects and people that he hoped could give him some insights into the murders of Zagan and Stalker, Forte still had absolutely nothing to go on. He kept asking himself who would want to murder the Vicar General and the Chancellor of the Archdiocese of Rosanada. Surely there had to be a connection between the two killings. His greatest fear was that the killer would strike again.

He had had a wonderful weekend with Miguel putting together a model of the Hindenburg. Of course he did most of the intricate work, but Miguel seemed delighted just to watch much of the time. The only problem he had about weekends with his son was that he had to return him to his mother every Sunday night.

"OK, Miguel, let's pack up your things. It is time to go." The boy dropped down on the floor beside the bed where his red suitcase was waiting for his things.

"I don't want to go. I want to stay here at home with you. I don't want to go to Gram's house," he protested. "Can't you get Mom to come back here?" Tears were beginning to form in his eyes, and he was struggling to control them.

Forte stuffed the boy's pajamas and his dirty clothes into the suitcase and zipped it up.

"I promised your mother that I would bring you to the Sunday evening Mass at Santiago Church and she would meet us there." The arrangement appealed to Forte, because at the Mass he would sit with his wife Anita and Miguel like a regular family and he could pretend that they would soon be united under one roof again.

When he arrived at Santiago, the parking lot was full and he had to park in the alley next to the church. Anita had already arrived and was waiting for them. Quickly he slipped into the pew with Miguel, gave her a quick kiss on the cheek, feeling her recoil and turn away from him at his touch.

He knelt to pray. It was always easy for him to pray at Santiago. An atmosphere of prayer surrounded him, as he knelt in the shadows before the altar. His eyes kept wandering until they rested on the tabernacle where the flickering red sanctuary candle spoke to him of peace. He still could not understand why the tabernacle had been removed from the altar and placed to the side. So many changes that had been made since Vatican II simply did not make sense to him. He figured that all the changes were probably responsible for the chaos that now existed in the Roman Catholic Church.

He had dropped out of the seminary after one year, because various members of the faculty were not following the traditional teachings of the Church, but were teaching their own views of theology. It had been unnerving to him, when he learned that his professor of Sacred Scripture, did not believe in anything miraculous, but had a natural explanation for everything. He insisted that when the Israelites fled from Egypt under the leadership of Moses, that they crossed the Red Sea at a time the water was very low, and they merely had to wade through a few inches of water. When he asked the professor how the entire Egyptian army managed to drown in just a few inches of water, as the Scripture said, he had no explanation for that.

His professor did not believe in the virgin birth of Christ, the slaughter of the Holy Innocents by Herod, the existence of the Magi, nor the feeding of the five thousand. He taught that the loaves and fishes were multiplied by everyone bringing out the lunches they had packed and brought with them. He believed that the bodily resurrection of Jesus never took place, and that it did not matter, because Christ was spiritually present with His people. He knew that St. Paul had taught that if Christ is not risen from the dead, then we are all still dead in our sins. When the professor insisted that no one believed in transubstantiation and that transignification was the correct dogma, Forte decided it was time to leave the seminary, before they destroyed his faith completely. No wonder priests were causing so much scandal in the Church. The seminaries were failing them, feeding them with pap and drivel instead of the Word of God and only the pure Word of God could make a man a faithful believer in Jesus Christ.

He loved to be with the people of God—they were the Church, not the hierarchy and the priests who were the cause of so much scandal. The simple faith of these people in the pews around him was strong. He could feel it, as he rested before the altar in Santiago. The traditional Spanish architecture spoke to him of the long line of churches the Spanish missionaries had built in America and of the faith of the people who had worked and saved to build them.

He prayed that the Church would be cleansed of false teaching and the faithless priests that such teaching fostered. "Lord, help me to bring Zagan's and Stalker's killer to justice." Most of all he prayed that his family would be reunited and that Anita would return to him. When the congregation began praying the Our Father, he reached over and tried to take Anita's hand in his, but she rebuffed him and stuck her hand hurriedly in the pocket of her gray slacks.

When the Mass was over, she grabbed Miguel by the hand and dragged him out of the pew after her and left without even saying goodbye.

Bright and early the next day, Forte headed for

the chancery to question a few more of the members on the staff there. At the top of his list was Monsignor Paul F.X. Linde, the promoter of justice, whom he had heard was a gay activist that even marched in gay parades.

"I am very busy," Detective, Linde protested when the secretary announced him to the promoter of justice. "I have important cases that I am working on right now." Rising to his feet and walking aggressively toward Forte, he forcefully asked, "What can I do for you?"

Forte could see at once that Linde had an in-your-face-attitude. The man was short—only about five and a half feet tall, but he put on a very macho performance —spitting out his words as he talked.

"I had hoped you could shed some light on the deaths of Zagan and Stalker" he stated, extending his hand to Linde who declined to respond to his overture of greeting.

Linde simply pointed to his desk that was covered with papers that Forte presumed to concern priests that were facing a canonical trial for which he would be the promoter of justice.

"I know nothing, absolutely nothing," he insisted. "And even if I did, I would not tell you without an attorney present. So you see, Detective, you are wasting my time and yours. Good day, Sir!" Linde opened his office door and waited for him to leave.

He did not like Linde. It was hard for Forte to

understand how a priest—the promoter of justice for the archdiocese—could be a gay activist.

Obviously L'Abbadon did not care, for he did nothing to censure him.

Next he determined to visit Father Minimo Tabron, who was currently assigned to a nursing home for the elderly at 13 Oblivion Lane in the very center of Daftmarsh, a withering little town near Rosanada. He had read the detailed accounts that Wayne Creasy, star reporter for the *Rosanada News*, had written about an allegation that a convicted felon and gay activist had made about Tabron, accusing him of sexually abusing him when he was still a minor ten years previously.

He had no trouble finding the nursing home, parked his unmarked police car, a white Chevy Impala, in the drive, rang the buzzer, and waited for someone to answer. A nun wearing an ugly black dress and short black veil opened the door and gruffly inquired, "Yes?"

"I would like to see Father Tabron. Would you tell him I am here, please?" He handed her his card which read "Cristian Forte, Rosanada Police, Homicide" and listed his phone number.

She stared at him fixedly and grunted, "Come in." He waited at least ten minutes in the waiting room of the nursing home for the priest to appear. Tabron, wearing black slacks and a T-shirt that revealed his muscular build, appeared to be in his sixties and seemed strong and robust. Clumsily—

91

he sat down in a chair across from him. "I am always glad to help the police," he stated.

"I am investigating the murders of Zagan and Stalker. Since you have been in the archdiocese for a long time, I thought perhaps you could be of help."

"I have never been privy to what goes on in the inner sanctum of the chancery. I can't imagine who would want to kill them." Tabron ran his fingers through his long shaggy gray hair. "It must have been someone that they had infuriated. They have closed a lot of parishes lately. Many people are disgruntled. Perhaps you witnessed the demonstrations at the funeral for Zagan?"

Forte nodded. "You were removed from your pastorate. Is that correct?"

"Yes, someone—a convicted felon—made accusations of sexual abuse against me. They removed me from my parish, and sent me here to this nursing home where half of the people don't know their left foot from their right. Alzheimer's, you understand." Tabron shifted nervously in his chair. His shifty grey eyes revealed a person who was ill at ease and deeply troubled.

Somewhere in the inner workings of the nursing home a phone rang insistently, but no one answered it.

"How much did the archdiocese pay your accuser?"

"Seventy-five thousand dollars and he did not even have to swear out a deposition. "L'Abbadon paid him with practically no questions asked," Tabron replied bitterly.

"Why do you suppose he paid him off so quickly and without a depo even being taken?"

"For years he has been shielding priests who were guilty of sexual abuse of minors and has been moving them from parish to parish. That is a felony. If he went on the witness stand, all that would come out. You see Rome sent out a directive that all sexual offenses of priests were to be squelched and never reported to the police. He was just following orders and now he does not dare answer questions about what he has done."

"What is the status of your case?" Forte asked him as he pulled his pipe from his coat pocket, tamped tobacco down in it, and lit it with a Ronson lighter. A cloud of sweet aromatic smoke engulfed him.

"There is absolutely no proof that I abused that kid," Minimo replied defiantly. "The promoter of justice has been investigating my case. No determination has been made yet. I'm still on the payroll, but I have lost my parish forever. They have assigned me to Happy Manor Home for the Elderly—a horrible assignment. L'Abbadon says he will never let me be a pastor again. They could defrock me. The archbishop will decide what course of action to take against me and the promoter of justice will enforce his decision."

"But aren't they required to have a canonical trial

to defrock you?"

"Yes, but L'Abbadon holds all the power and control in his hands. He will decide the outcome of the trial. Probably already has. They will merely rubberstamp his decision, and he has already determined I will never be a pastor again." Tabron folded his hands in his lap and twiddled his thumbs. Suddenly he slapped his palms down on his thighs and clumsily rose to his feet. "You will have to excuse me now. I have to anoint a patient who is dying."

Seeing that he could get no more information from Tabron, he said, "Well, if you think of anything that might help solve these crimes, give me a call. Thanks for your time, Father." As he was leaving the nursing home, he made the decision to put a tail on Tabron to see if he might lead him to something that would help break the case open.

In the days that followed, he learned that Father Tabron was often a visitor at Frankie's Bar, if fact even had a small apartment over the bar on the third floor of the building. Furthermore, he was often seen there in the company of one Gautier d'Arras, a young Haitian, who also lived over Frankie's, and to whom he appeared to serve as mentor. Forte decided he would have to pay a visit to Frankie's bar and check it out for himself.

14

Pompeo

Having an apartment over Frankie's Bar probably had some advantages for Minimo. He never liked to be alone and anytime he wanted company he could go downstairs to the bar and find friends. The rent was probably all he could afford on the stipend they were paying for taking care of inmates at the nursing home in Daftmarsh. Although they gave him a room there, he said he wanted a place of his own where he could have privacy away from the prying eyes of the nuns and where he could entertain his friends. No doubt he missed the large rectory and staff he had at St. Joan of Arc and the wonderful meals the cook prepared for him there, but he maintained that he was quite comfortable now.

To get to Minimo's third-floor apartment, Pompeo entered by a dark and dingy stairway located behind the bar in Frankie's. Minimo had invited him to spend the evening with him and Gautier d'Arras, who had a large apartment on the fourth floor and who had become a good friend. Apparently Minimo liked the young Haitian considerably, because he spent a lot of time with him, whenever he could get away from the nursing home. Oh, well, thought Pompeo, Minimo was probably better off here than he was living at St.

Popola's, under the supervision of Zagan before his murder, and now Bishop Morales, and John Bugumil, who had moved into Zagan's old suite.

He looked forward to visiting Minimo. They had been friends since seminary days and he enjoyed his company, even though Minimo tended to be sloppy and clumsy.

As soon as he entered Frankie's bar, he thought he saw Monsignor Linde in the crowd over in one corner talking to someone he did not recognize. He decided to ask Minimo about it.

"When I came in through Frankie's bar, I thought I saw Monsignor Linde and perhaps Monsignor Finolli in the crowd over in the corner dancing. Was that them?" Pompeo asked with surprise written on his face.

"Of, course. They are here almost every night and always on the weekends." Minimo replied, grinning at Pompeo who seemed shocked.

"They were wearing gay pride shirts." Pompeo exclaimed dubiously.

"Of course, you did not know?"

"Well, like they always say. It takes one to know one. I am not gay."

"Let's forget them and go upstairs to Gautier's apartment. He is expecting us." Minimo led the way up the dark and dingy stairway to the fourth floor. "I think you will find him fascinating, Pompeo, since you are interested in various cultures and in cultural anthropology. He has turned his apartment into a peristyle—a voodoo temple. He is a *Bokor—houngan* who practices Petro Voodoo, or black magic. Later this evening, he is going to hold a ceremony, when his *serviteurs* and members of his group arrive. In fact, he is going to have a *wanga* for me," Minimo explained with obvious enthusiasm.

"A *wanga?*"

"Yeah, it is like a curse. He is making a doll to represent L'Abaddon."

"A voodoo doll?" Pompeo asked with an expression of disgust.

"Yes, it will make L'Abbadon change his attitude toward us and reinstate us is our parishes as pastors again."

"How much did you have to pay him for that" Pompeo asked cynically.

"Seventy-five dollars. He had to get his sister Josette who works as L'Abbadon's maid to bring him some hair from the archbishop's brush and comb. Of course, she had to be paid. He is putting L'Abbadon's hair in the *wanga* doll—that is what makes the spell work." Minimo's face beamed with fervor.

Remembering how Minimo had spent two years in a mental institution for schizophrenia while in Europe, Pompeo shook his head in dismay and followed his friend as they emerged on the fourth floor.

When they entered Gautier's apartment, Pompeo was surprised by what he saw. He had obviously entered a temple or shrine of some kind.

"Good evening," Gautier welcomed them, inviting them to sit on cushions on the floor, while he walked into the adjoining room where Pompeo could see an altar that was draped with a white cloth held down by four highly polished black stones— one at each corner.

"Excuse me," he said, "I will be with you in a moment. I was just getting some things ready for the services." He had a crystal bowl in his hands that he proceeded to fill with water and three splashes of dark Caribbean rum.

Pompeo watched as Gautier carefully put some earth and a bit of salt into a glass candleholder. After rubbing a tall white candle with olive oil, he inserted it firmly into the candleholder and placed it in front of the bowl of water on the altar.

"As soon as I put fresh flowers and some jewelry around the bowl, I will be right with you," Gautier explained. Then, pointing to the elaborate fuschia and gold sequined banner that hung on the wall above the altar, he asked, "How do you like my new *dwapo*. I just finished making it today."

"It is very lovely," Pompeo remarked. "Whose pictures are on the altar and on the wall behind it?"

"They are the *loas*, the special spirits that I honor.

This is Erzulie," he said, pointing to a statue of a woman that was about two feet tall and stood to the left of the altar. Surprisingly, her skin was light in tone. Her long black hair hung straight down to her shoulders, one of which was bare and the other draped in a manner that resembled the way in which Romans wore the toga. On her head she wore a crown decorated with gems in red and green. Her blue gown that reached to the floor, but still revealed her bare feet, left one leg exposed from the knee down.

"Every peristyle has a special place for her. She is the most beloved of the *loas*. She represents our dreams, hopes and aspirations. And she is very sorrowful and weeps a lot. We associate her with the Virgin Mary. Her symbol is a heart with a broken arrow in it," Gautier explained. "We are Catholics, you know. We go to Mass on Sunday, same as you."

"You are Catholic?" asked Pompeo with surprise.

"*Mais oui, mon père.*" Gautier insisted as he smiled warmly at Pompeo.

"I don't know anything about Voodoo," Pompeo replied, as he took a sip of the sweet purple wine that Gautier handed him.

"It is really fascinating," Minimo said anxious to share what he had already learned about Gautier and his religion. "In Haiti where Gautier is from, 80 percent of the people are Catholic and 100 per cent practice Voodoo. Aristide made it an official religion of Haiti in 2003. They believe in God, *le Bon Dieu* or *Bondye*, as they call the deity, whom they believe is too busy with the universe to bother about them. So they usually start their services with a prayer to *Bondye* and then seek to establish contact with the *loas*, the spirits, which are very much like Catholic saints. You see, the early French settlers tried to stamp out the African religion which is still practiced by about sixty million people worldwide. So to preserve their religion they identified their ancestral spirits with the Catholic saints."

Looking at the statue of the seated man in black at the right of the altar, Pompeo asked, "Who is he?" He was intrigued by the bizarre statue of the man with a black cross and a tomb in front of him.

"Yes," urged Minimo, "tell us about him."

"He is Papa Ghede—the spirit of death. He is the power behind the magic that kills!" Gautier's voice took on a sinister timbre as he spoke of Ghede. "He controls the souls of all who meet death as a result of Petro Voodoo."

"A somber figure," commented Pompeo.

"He is also the *loa* of sex. When he appears at a ceremony and takes possession of someone, he is always horny like a goat. He is also a clown who is constantly joking, making erotic jokes."

As Gautier refilled their wine glasses, a very dark-skinned man came out of Gautier's bedroom. He moved lethargically and seemed to be taken up in his thoughts and completely oblivious to his surroundings and was not even aware that he and Minimo were there.

"*Bon soir*, Didier," Gautier said to the newcomer.

"Meet my friends Minimo and Pompeo." The dark-skinned man moved mechanically across the room and stood right in front of them, nodded and sat down next to Gautier without speaking a word. He seemed to be only half awake.

"Didier is a zombie," Gautier explained. My father made him into a zombie about five years ago and gave him to me when I came to this country."

"I find that hard to believe," Pompeo protested, as he put his empty wine glass down on the floor beside him and waited for Gautier to refill it. "You are joking with me. There is no such thing as a zombie." He waved his hands in front of his face in a negative gesture.

"Can you tell us, Gautier?" asked Minimo how zombies are made."

Minimo was staring intently at Didier who did not seem to move a muscle, but sat like an automaton waiting for Gautier's command. A large black tomcat came running out from the bedroom and jumped up on Didier's lap, but the zombie seemed not to be aware of the cat's presence.

"*Viens, Luci!*" Gautier called the cat to himself. Settling down at Gautier's feet, the cat purred so loudly that they could all hear him. With his dark green eyes, he stared suspiciously at Pompeo to whom the animal seemed evil. He imagined that his wild purring could quickly turn to hisses, if he were disturbed.

"Do you have the *wanga* doll ready?" Minimo asked eagerly.

"Yes, it is all ready except for putting some of L'Abbadon's hair in it. My sister Josette brought me some that she collected from his hairbrush and comb this afternoon. I will do that now," he replied going into the room where the altar stood.

"Come in here with me, *mes amis*," Gautier invited, as he stuffed L'Abbadons gray hair into the body of a doll that was about six inches long and resembled nothing human with its crude face and lumpy body.

"What's a *wanga?*" Pompeo asked as he joined them in the room with the altar.

"It is a spell to compel L'Abbadon to change his attitude toward us."

"You mean it is a curse?"

"You might say that."

"I don't believe in that sort of thing. I am not superstitious," Pompeo protested.

Minimo came to the defense of his friend. "Gautier is a *Bokor*, a witch doctor, and he has a good track record with *wangas*. His father was a *houngan bokor* of *Petro Voodoo* and he has been teaching him since he was a little child. He has had all three priestly initiations and is fully qualified." Minimo seemed proud of his friend's accomplishments.

Not convinced, Pompeo stated flatly, "I have always taken an interest in cultural things and cultural anthropology, so I find what you do is interesting." With his back to Gautier so that only Minimo could observe him, Pompeo shook his head in disbelief and rolled his eyes upward and became silent.

When Minimo saw this gesture and to justify his bringing Pompeo to a voodoo ceremony, he commented, "I want to remind you that Pope John Paul II was photographed with a voodoo priest at his ecumenical meeting in Assisi in 1986."

Not convinced, Pompeo trailed behind as Gautier led them into a smaller adjoining room. Obviously it was the inner sanctum that housed all Gautier's voodoo accoutrements. Actually this room reminded Pompeo of a sacristy.

"I will show you how powerful voodoo is, Pompeo, and you will no longer doubt me," Gautier boasted confidently, as he walked over to a table on which were arranged all manner of strange, grotesque, and even sinister things— crystals, feathers, and a rattle made of a gourd. Picking up the rattle, Gautier explained that it was the *asson*. "See it is covered with snake bones and bits of coral. I will use it to summon the *loas*—the spirits who will enter the bodies of the *serviteurs*, when the ceremony begins in about an hour, when the folks arrive."

Pompeo was fascinated by the strange and exotic assortment of objects on the table before him. He picked up the brightly painted red and black *asson* and gave it a shake. The rattling of the seeds inside the gourd sounded like the hissing of a snake. A human skull—obviously authentic—sat in the middle of the table. It had been made into a grotesque candle holder. Deftly Gautier inserted a burning stick into one of the empty eye sockets of the skull and lit the candle which began to flicker ominously creating eerie shadows. Sitting beside the skull was a large glass bowl that contained a fat and warty toad that seemed to be watching them with its small beady eyes.

What attracted Minimo's attention was the skull of an alligator that sat on the table next to the human skull. Then his eyes lit on the many colored bottles that lined the back portion of the table and all of which bore a skull and cross bones on their front surfaces except for a plain red bottle. As he reached over to pick up one of the blue bottles, Gautier abruptly cautioned, "Careful!"

Minimo quickly withdrew his hand without touching any of the bottles.

"If you do not know how to use them, they are deadly poison, except for the red bottle which just contains a sleeping potion. And pointing to a group of the blue bottles, he said, "They are the most powerful poison of all of them."

Pompeo smiled knowingly at Minimo, displaying his unbelief. Seeing that Pompeo considered him to be a charlatan, Gautier said, "Look here. I will give you a demonstration of their lethal power."

Before proceeding with his exhibition, Gautier opened a bottle containing some acrid oil and rubbed it carefully on his hands, face and arms, saying that it was to protect him from the lethal effects of the contents of the blue bottle that he very carefully opened. Then taking the toad from the glass bowl, he set it on the table in front of him. Being extremely careful not to get the white powder from the blue bottle on his skin or to breathe in any of the dust arising from the powder, he sprinkled some of it very carefully on the toad.

"Watch the toad," he directed as the animal began to quiver and shake and lose its balance. Within minutes it was motionless, flopped over on its back with its feet in the air—completely lifeless.

Pompeo was utterly amazed at the demonstration of the effectiveness of the poison.

"What is that poison?" Minimo asked in astonishment.

"It is a neuro poison from the puffer fish—one of the most deadly poisons known to man," Gautier explained. "It is the one we use to turn a man into a zombie. After he is dead about three days and even buried—no visible heartbeat or respiration—we revive him. He becomes a virtual slave of the *houngan* who made him. He is brain dead, but he can function like Didier, who is still sitting out there waiting for me to command him."

"You expect us to believe that?" Pompeo, always

the skeptic, asked.

"Watch and see." Gautier took one of the green bottles from the table in front of him and carefully opened it up and poured some of its contents on the dead toad. Slowly the toad began to breathe as they watched spellbound. The creature opened one eye and then the other, as Gautier reached down, picked him up, and set him on his feet. Suddenly the toad jumped across the table and in three hops was on the floor where Gautier scurried to recapture him and return him to his glass bowl.

"Sure," said Pompeo, "that is easy to do with a creature like a toad—a simple life form. Let me ask—if you had not put the powder from the green bottle on the toad, he would have remained dead?"

"Of course, it is very powerful poison. In Haiti we use it to make zombies. It destroys brain function," Gautier answered.

"Zombies?" scoffed Pompeo. "There are no such things as zombies. Try that on a more complex animal and I would be more inclined to believe you. Try it on your tomcat."

"No problem, man." Gautier seemed delighted to rise to the challenge. He ran his hand through the forest of pigtails that covered his large skull. His thick purplish lips burst into a big smile as he called *"Luci, viens ici!"*

Immediately the black cat came running and began rubbing its head on Gautier's bare ankle just below his blue jeans.

"You call that cat Luci? That is a female name and he is a tomcat?" asked the ever incredulous Pompeo as his eyes questioned the *houngan*.

"Ah, *mon père*," Gautier exclaimed, "his name is really Lucifer."

Intently Minimo and Pompeo watched as Gautier picked up the cat, set him on the table, while the cat continued purring loudly and began licking Gautier's very black hand.

Pompeo was amazed as Gautier poured the white powder from the blue bottle on the head of the cat, noting that some of the powder fell into the cat's eyes, and he could not help breathing in sizeable amounts of it. Within seconds the cat, sitting on the table, began to lose muscular control, with his front legs beginning to twitch. Apparently attacked with vertigo, the cat looked dazed and fell over on his side. His long black tail went completely rigid and the animal began to gasp for breath.

"Stop!" cried Minimo. "Enough. No need to make the cat suffer anymore. Give him the antidote from the green bottle now."

Quickly Gautier applied the antidote over the head of the cat who was now lying lifeless on the table before him. "Wake up Luci," he commanded as he rubbed the cat's head and ears.

Pompeo and Minimo watched as life began returning to the cat. Even though the animal opened his eyes, they remained lifeless in appearance. Although he got up and stood on all four feet, he seemed to be still in a daze.

"Now we have a zombie cat," Gautier said with a laugh as his gold earrings jangled against his strong masculine jowls. He carried the dazed animal into the main room of the peristyle where Didier was still sitting lifelessly waiting for Gautier's orders and asked him to take care of Lucifer.

"Come," Gautier called to Minimo and Pompeo who were still in the back room. "It is time for the members to arrive and to begin the ceremony." He threw open the entrance door to his apartment. And within minutes the first five people arrived. After brief introductions three of the men—all dark-skinned Haitians who had brought drums with them—assembled in a corner of the peristyle and began to beat their jungle rhythms softly but insistently, while Gautier pulled on a red flowing gown over his blue jeans and T-shirt.

When about twenty men had assembled in the room, Gautier went to the center of the room to the *poteau-mitan,* a pole around which the members would dance when the *houngan* would begin shaking the *asson* to call down the *loas*—the spirits. He began by spreading white cloths on the floor within the circle of believers who were seated around the room. Slowly and with great care he began creating the *vévé* by pouring out cornmeal creating an intricate design dedicated to Erzulie and Papa Ghede on the white fabric.

Pompeo was seated next to Minimo and

opposite the altar on which Gautier had placed the *wanga* doll that he had made containing L'Abbadon's hair. When the two of them were able to converse together quietly without anyone overhearing them, Pompeo nudged Minimo gently and commented, "There are no women here. They are all men."

Minimo chuckled softly. "That is because this peristyle has all gay members. Voodoo does not discriminate against people because of their sexual orientation."

Having finished making the *vévé*, Gautier stood in front of his altar, lit the candle, picked up a long staff that was decorated with blue and white feathers, a few small bones, and a few trailing ribbons, and began the ceremony with a long prayer to *Bondye*. When he had finished this he said a Hail Mary to which all those present responded vociferously. Four *serviteurs*, all dressed in white robes, were standing in attendance upon Gautier, who had laid aside the long feather staff and was picking up the *asson*. This seemed to be a cue to the drummers, for they began beating their drums more insistently and louder.

Pompeo watched as Gautier, shaking his *asson*, and the *serviteurs*, shuffling their feet, began dancing around the *poteau-mitan*, while chanting a plaintiff song. With greater and greater fury, Gautier shook the *asson* and the *serviteurs* were joined in the dance by the various members who were eager to participate. The *hougnan* was now holding a large red rooster in his hands, as he whirled and spun around the *poteau-mitan*. Pompeo noticed that the roosters legs had been tied together to immobilize him. He also suspected that they had given the bird something to tranquilize him.

As the drums reached a crescendo, Gautier took a knife from the pocket of his blood red garment and slit the rooster's throat. Holding the bleeding rooster over his head, he let the animal's blood run into his open mouth. Then he held the rooster over the *wanga* doll containing hair from L'Abbadon and let the blood saturate it.

Faster and faster went the drums. Gautier was chanting in Creole in an eerie high-pitched voice, as he danced around the pole in the center of the room. He swayed and spun on his feet, while clapping his hands ferociously to the beat of the drums. Suddenly one of the *serviteurs* cried out in a frenzy "Papa Ghede is here," as he undulated sensuously over the *vévé* that was becoming obliterated by the feet of the dancers.

"Papa Ghede, welcome!" cried the dancers. Their dancing became more and more sensuous as their bare feet kept up with the fury of the drums. Some of the men cast off their shirts that had become saturated with perspiration from the frenetic activity of the dance. Their ebony skin glistened in the subdued light of the peristyle.

Pompeo, determined not to participate in the ceremony in any way, remained seated with Minimo, while noticing that one of the dancers, the one who first cried out, "Papa Ghede" was wearing dark glasses, but strangely the glass on the right side had been broken and was missing. He was making suggestive gestures to the other dancers.

"Look Minimo," Pompeo exclaimed, as he saw that the dancing was becoming more voluptuous and erotic. "It is getting late. I have to go now." He had had enough, more than enough!

Without waiting for his response, Pompeo rose to his feet and ran to the door, slipped out into the hall and made his way down the darkly lit staircase and emerged into Frankie's bar where the all male patrons were dancing with almost as much gusto as those he had just seen upstairs. Through the smoky haze he could see Monsignor Linde dancing sensuously with someone he could not recognize.

As he drove home to his small room at St. Popola's, he kept remembering how Minimo had spent two years in a mental institution in Europe because of schizophrenia. Obviously, he was still crazy. He certainly had no intention of ever being in the company of Gautier d'Arras again. The very idea—voodoo gays. He could not understand why Minimo would want to associate with such people. No wonder the archbishop had told him he was not fit to be a pastor of a congregation. What would Minimo possibly do next?

15

Renato

Fear had settled over the archiepiscopal residence like a dark and blinding miasma. It was as if a coiled cobra hid in the darkness waiting to strike, when they least expected it. Both he and L'Abbadon carried their Berettas with them constantly, ready to use them upon the least provocation or threat. Terror stalked them constantly ever since Stalker had died in L'Abbadon's office shortly after the archbishop had left him for the night.

Renato could not believe that the archbishop had killed Stalker. He had no reason to— absolutely no motive—as far as he could determine. However, he had to admit that L'Abbadon was probably a top suspect of the Rosanada Police Department. Glancing out the window of his room, Renato could see the patrol car parked in front of the mansion. Thank God, the security system was set and if anyone breached it, a loud alarm would sound.

At supper, served informally in the breakfast room off the kitchen, L'Abbadon seemed deeply agitated with his lips pursed in a circle, eating silently, while glancing furtively around him, as if expecting some insidious evil to suddenly appear and engulf him.

"Who could have wanted to kill Stalker?" he asked with a rasping voice. His hand trembled as he cut his filet. Although Josette had prepared an excellent meal with the help of André who acted as chef and butler, L'Abbadon only picked at his food.

Renato made no attempt to answer his question.

"They really want me, you know." L'Abbadon's voice was muffled and uncertain as he spoke. "Why would anyone want to kill me?" he whined as he took a sip of a ten year old imported Bordeau.

Renato was not very hungry either, but managed to finish off the steak and two glasses of wine.

Impetuously L'Abbadon pushed his chair back from the table and rose to his feet. "Let's play Gin Rummy in my room tonight, Renato." He walked cautiously around the indoor pool that separated the dining room from the living room and went into the den and opened a box of his special reserve Cuban cigars that he obtained illegally from a shady tobacconist in the lower east side of Rosanada. After offering him one, L'Abbadon lit the cigar with a golden lighter that he kept in his pocket. The cloud of smoke seemed to relax him as they made their way back to the living room. When they passed before the great painting of the archbishop in all his regalia, L'Abbadon paused before his portrait and assumed the same stance as in the painting with hands held outstretched one upon the other. Seeing himself self-assured, calm, and beaming with good cheer lifted his spirits. One by one he blew out the candles that flamed in the pair of three branched golden Florentine candlesticks that stood one on each side of the portrait that reached from ceiling to floor. Slowly he turned off the spotlights that illuminated the painting, uttered a deep sigh, and headed for his room.

"Come, Renato. I will beat you at Gin. Twenty-five cents a point, OK?"

When they entered "L'Abbadon's bedroom, the pet poodle, Pigalle, that was curled up on the lavender moiré bedspread on L'Abbadon's bed growled ever so slightly at having her rest disturbed.

L'Abbadon put up a card table, searched through his highboy dresser until he found playing cards, pen and paper. Somewhere in the deep recesses of the house a door slammed. Renato saw the way L'Abbadon jumped in fear at the noise. Going into his walk-in closet, he found there a bottle of Scotch and a couple of glasses. Quickly he poured two drinks and drank his down in one gulp and poured himself another.

Holding Pigalle on his lap, L'Abbadon began dealing out the cards. In the distance they could here the siren of a police car in the night. The wail of the siren sent chills down Renato's back.

He found it hard to play cards. L'Abbadon was beating him at every hand. He always managed to get gin when he held a handful of cards. Pigalle stirred restlessly on L'Abbadon's lap.

"I think he wants to go out, Renato. I'll ring for André to take him out." L'Abbadon glanced at his Rolex. "It is already ten o'clock and André and Josette have already gone for the night. I guess you will have to take him out, Renato, but hurry I don't want to stay here alone any longer than necessary." L'Abbadon handed him the poodle and a leash.

Renato made his way down through the darkened house that was as quiet as a mausoleum now that the staff had gone for the day. He decided to take the dog out the front where the police car was stationed. With his Baretta in his right hand and the dog on his left arm, he cautiously opened the heavy door with its crystal panes.

"Good evening, officers," he called to the police in the squad car.

"Anything wrong?" they called back.

"No. Just taking the dog for his evening outing." It was a comfort to have the men in blue there.

When he returned into the silent house, reset the security system, and climbed the stairs to L'Abbadon's chamber, the archbishop was agitated. He quickly locked his bedroom door behind Renato after he came in.

"You will sleep in my room tonight, Renato. don't want to be alone. Here is a pair of my pajamas." L'Abbadon handed him a pair of his lavender pajamas, pulled down the covers and jumped into bed.

In the mirror on the ceiling over the king-sized bed, Renato could see the archbishop fingering an ivory rosary, while he muttered his prayers under his breath. Just as he was about to drift off to sleep, the jangling noise of the telephone, brought them both to sudden awareness.

"Answer the phone, Renato." L'Abbadon commanded gruffly in rasping tones.

"Del'Ano here," he said.

"This is Detective Forte from homicide. I just phoned to alert you and the archbishop that someone tried to kill Monsignor Finolli about an hour ago."

"What happened?" Renato asked filled with dread.

"He was walking from his car to his apartment in the parking lot behind his condo on Water Street when someone in the darkness fired a shot at him. The bullet put a hole in his hat, but he was unharmed. Fortunately, he got into his condo before a second shot was fired."

"Do you have any suspects?" Renato asked nervously as he tapped his fingers on the table beside the bed.

"None, but I called to warn you and L'Abbadon to be especially careful all the time, but especially at night. You never know who might be lurking in the bushes." The detective said good night wishing them both well.

"What happened?" L'Abbadon asked with fear

written over his features.

"Someone tired to kill Monsignor Finolli tonight. Took a shot at him and put a whole through his Fedora. He is all right. The detective phoned to warn us to be very careful. The killer might strike again and not miss a second time."

Fear stricken, L'Abbadon resumed saying the rosary while pulling up the blankets over his head. After a few minutes when Renato felt him tapping him on his left shoulder, he pretended to be asleep. Although the tapping became more insistent and demanding, he refused to acknowledge it. Finally L'Abbadon yelled at him, "Wake up, Renato. I need you."

Without trying to hide his feelings of annoyance, he replied "What do you want? It is late and I want to go to sleep."

"Hear my confession," L'Abbadon whined pitifully.

"You know I cannot do that, because of our relationship," he protested as he rolled over turning his back on him. Then in an attempt to calm the prelate and assuage his fears, he added, "Just pray to God. Confess to Him."

"I can't," L'Abbadon wailed. "I can't find Him. I don't know where to find Him," he moaned pursing his lips in a grimace. "He never listens to my prayers no matter how many Our Fathers and Hail Marys I say." His voice rose to a high pitched screech as he continued pleading for help. "They are going to kill me! I can feel it!"

"You are perfectly safe here. There is a cop car outside and we have our Berettas. See here is mine right under the pillow. I won't let anyone hurt you." Renato tried to soothe his fears.

L'Abbadon grabbed him by the shoulder. "Turn over and look at me," he commanded. He rolled over and lay facing L'Abbadon whose twisted and flushed face displayed the terror the prelate was experiencing. L'Abbadon's bloodshot eyes were pleading for help.

"Does hell exist, Renato?" he moaned.

"You have always insisted that it does not, Your Excellency."

"Well, what do you think, Renato?"

"You know I always agree with you in everything. As you have so often said—you make the rules in Rosanada."

"Yes, yes, of course. Give me a shot to put me to sleep," he ordered imperiously. "You are right. I make the rules here."

Renato rose from the bed, went into the adjoining bathroom, found the diazepam and returned with the syringe filled with a heavy dose of the tranquilizer. After he administered it to L'Abbadon, his wailing subsided. "I need a glass of Scotch, please, Renato," he begged.

Renato retrieved the bottle of Scotch from the liquor cabinet opposite the bed, poured some into a glass and gave it to L'Abbadon who took it with a shaking hand and quaffed it, collapsing back on the bed.

Sleep did not come easily to Renato. Somewhere in the night a dog howled mournfully—a dreadful sound that chilled his blood. When would all this end, he wondered, as he fell asleep dreaming of snakes.

16

Forte

He had to get the killer, before he struck again. The attempt on the life of Monsignor Finolli was a bold move on the part of the man who had killed Zagan and Stalker. There was no doubt in his mind that it was the same man who attacked all three, and he was also certain that the assassin would strike again. Finolli had parked his car in the lot behind his condo about ten the previous evening. He was coming home from a party at the home of Monsignor Linde when, shortly after he got out of his car and started walking towards the Chantilly where he had a condo on the third floor, he spotted someone moving in the shadows on his left. Apprehensive because of the murders of Zagan and Stalker, he ducked behind a van and was attempting to cross the short distance to the building when he heard a shot ring out, but missing him. Then a second shot rang out and a bullet went right through his hat. A few inches lower and he would be dead.

Determined to leave no stone unturned in his search for the killer, he kept visiting and interviewing everyone that could possibly be considered a suspect. That morning he had visited three priests who had been pastors of parishes that had been closed permanently, because their Sunday collections did not pay the bills, and L'Abbadon adamantly refused to subsidize them or loan them any more money to keep them afloat. Now he was on his way to see Father Patrick Flynn, parochial vicar at St. Brigid's on Shady Lane. Recently the *Rosanada News* carried a front page story of how Flynn was suing the archdiocese, claiming that he was discriminated against because he was not gay.

When he arrived at St. Brigid's rectory, he rang the bell and waited for what seemed an interminable amount of time before the housekeeper, a slovenly Irish woman with gray hair pulled up in a bun, answered the door with a broom in her hand. "Yes?" she asked, seemingly annoyed that he had rung the bell.

"I would like to see, Father Flynn." He pulled out his police badge and flashed it at the woman. "Detective Forte," he said flatly.

"Well, come in then." She led him into a waiting room that was austerely decorated in Sears Roebuck modern—a desk, a few straight back chairs, an armchair, and a sofa. There was a large crucifix on the wall behind the desk on which sat a clock that was chiming the half hour.

"He will be here in a few minutes" she said pushing back wisps of gray hair that had fallen loose from the bun. "I'll fetch him."

When she left the room, he looked around for a magazine or a newspaper to read while he waited. He found the *Rosanada News*. The morning paper had all the details of the attempt on the life of Monsignor Finolli. Wayne Creasy, star reporter, reveled in sensational stories of murder and mayhem. After reading the front page, he turned to the sports page and was just settling into it, when Father Flynn, a very sober looking young priest dressed in a clerical black suit and white Roman collar, opened the door and entered the waiting room.

"I'm Father Flynn," he said without showing any emotion of any kind. "What can I do for you? Please be seated," he invited as he took his seat behind the desk.

Sitting down in the armchair next to the desk, Forte showed him his police badge. "Detective Forte, Cristian Forte of the Rosanada Police, Homicide Division."

"I am afraid I have to ask you some questions, Father Flynn." The priest was sitting beneath an old painting of Pope Leo XIII that was dark and dingy and gave the entire room a somber tone.

"I don't see how I can help you, Detective. I don't know anything about the murders of Monsignors Zagan and Stalker." The priest's eyes were cold and assessing him.

"That is not what I want to discuss with you. I read about your lawsuit against the archbishop as a corporation sole asking for compensation for taking away your faculties and your stipend. I understand another priest has been assigned here at St. Brigid's and has taken over your duties, while you continue to live here. Is that correct?"

"Yes," Flynn responded softly causing Forte to lean forward in his chair to hear him more clearly. "I have been deprived of employment by my employer and I am seeking relief from the courts."

"Do you have any idea why L'Abbadon has put you on leave, while insisting that you continue living here?"

"The pastor Monsignor O' Neil has a friend, a priest from another diocese, who comes here and spends a week at a time. The man is an obvious gay. I complained to the archbishop about the relationship that Monsignor O'Neil has with him, a Father Jim Green. I found it disgusting to see the two of them together holding hands, and God only knows what they did in the pastor's room behind closed doors where Green spent the night." Father Flynn sighed deeply and looked at him to see if he understood what he was going through.

"So what did L'Abbadon say to you?" Forte asked as he looked at the priest sympathetically.

"He told me to go stay in a hotel whenever Green comes to visit." Flynn shook his head sadly. "I don't understand what has become of the Church." He slouched in his chair, propped his elbows on the desk, and rested his head in the palms of his hands. "All this was in the newspaper."

"Is there anything else?"

"Yes, I am suing him for retaliation. Because I complained about the relationship of my pastor and Green, he put me on leave and is demanding that I go to the Bachus and Sergius Institute in New Orleans for psychological evaluation. This is purely punitive. I have heard from other priests who have gone there and the treatment they have received was horrible and dehumanizing." Father Flynn folded his hands in front of him on the desk and looked dejected. "I didn't become a priest to endure such treatment. I am afraid L'Abbadon is trying to force me out of the priesthood."

"I am very sorry to hear your story. I had always wanted to be a priest. I spent a year at St. Gabriel's Seminary in Arborville. I am glad that I dropped out. I would probably be in the same boat you are in, if I had not." He shook Father Flynn's hand and wished him well and headed to his mother's house for dinner.

Since he and Anita had been separated, Juanita, his mother, invited him to dinner every Wednesday evening. His parent's home was always a place of refuge for him. His father Rodrigo Forte had retired from the practice of criminal law about a year before and understood fully what the life of a homicide detective was like.

When he arrived for dinner, the house was full of the fragrance of home baked bread just out of the oven. His mother had prepared *arroz con pollo* and lots of fresh salad, and vegetables just the way he liked them, and home made strawberry ice cream with chocolate cake for desert.

After dinner, his father opened the Bible and began the family devotions, as he always had, as far back as Cristian could remember. He read a passage from the gospels that showed the great mercy of Christ in dealing with sinners. Afterwards his mother, who had developed a devotion to St. Faustina, began reciting the Chaplet of the Divine Mercy.

Forte felt comfort in praying with his family. "Eternal Father, I offer You the Body and Blood, Soul and Divinity of Your dearly beloved Son, Our Lord Jesus Christ, in atonement for our sins and those of the whole world." He thought of the sins of the people of Rosanada and then multiplied them by the millions of people around the world and tried to grasp something of the magnitude of sin. With profound feeling and sincerity, he repeated the responses to his mother's prayers. When the chaplet concluded with "Holy God, Holy Mighty One, Holy Immortal One, have mercy on us and on the whole world," he sighed deeply and said, "The amazing mercy of God! How much we in the Church need it today."

His mother smiled at him and said, "You seem a bit depressed tonight, Son."

"Yes, all the corruption in the Church devastates

me. Gay priests! Murder right in the chancery and in the archbishop's residence! Church closings! Pope Julius III seminary shut down! No wonder only 25 per cent of the people attend Mass now. I have even heard that many gay priests are dabbling into the black arts— having Black Masses." He looked to his mother and father for some answers to the things that were disturbing him.

His father, who was on the church council at Santiago, leaned back in his chair, propped up his feet on the footstool and commented. "The Church is a divine institution. You just proved that with what you said."

"I don't understand," Cristian replied warming his back at the fireplace of the cozy living room.

"If the Church were not a divine institution," Rodrigo commented, "we would have killed it long ago. Any institution that can survive all the evils you mentioned has to be divine. There is no other explanation. Christ has promised that the gates of hell will never prevail against her and He has kept that promise for two thousand years. She has survived wicked popes, cardinals, and scandals in the priesthood."

"I never thought about it that way before, I see your point," Cristian said as he reached over and put another log on the fire.

"Yes, we have always known that, dear," his mother said, as she picked up her knitting and began rocking gently to and fro. "It is really sad when priests and bishops lose their faith and fall into evil, especially when they give scandal to the Church."

"It is always a temptation to think of the hierarchy as being the Church, but they aren't. The people of God are the Church and their faith has shone in the darkness down through the centuries. There always have been and always will be faithful holy souls among the people of God, even if they are only a small remnant, and they prevent God's wrath from striking down evil doers. Look at the saints—you will see them everywhere if you look for them. They are the people who keep the world together—the selfless ones who minister to the sick and the dying, who care for the orphans and widows, and who filled with the Holy Spirit send up incessant prayers of adoration to the Triune God." Rodrigo picked up his pipe and filled it with a fragrant rich tobacco.

"Yes," Juanita chimed in, "the people of God are people like your sister Carla and her husband Roberto and their three children. The children reflect the faith of their parents in their happy faces."

Cristian felt his spirits lift, as he considered what Rodrigo and Juanita told him. As he sat letting the peace of his parents' presence and home flood his soul, the cell phone in his pocket began to jangle.

"Forte here," he said into the phone, a bit annoyed that his peace had been disturbed.

"This is Chief Detective Conway. I need you

right away. There has been another murder. Monsignor Paul Linde was murdered behind Frankie's bar over on Second Street. The cop on the beat, Officer Casey, just reported hearing a shot and then finding Linde dead behind Frankie's. I want you to get over there immediately. I am sending the team to seal off the crime area, take the photos, and when you give the word, to remove the monsignor's body to the morgue."

"Right away, Chief." He snapped his phone shut and stuck it in his trouser's pocket. "I have to go, sorry." He left without telling his parents that another chancery priest, the promoter of justice, had just been murdered.

When he arrived at the scene, the forensic team was already there and had roped off the area. Curiosity seekers were pushing in as close as they could to get a glimpse of the corpse of the dead priest. Flash bulbs popped as forensics caught all the grisly details on film.

Forte could see that Linde had been shot in the head and had probably died instantly. The bullet appeared to have penetrated his left temple where a jagged wound was still bleeding. He was wearing a pair of faded blue jeans with holes at the knees and a faded lavender T shirt with a rainbow on it.

The officer in charge of forensics came over to where he was standing next to the body in the parking lot, about fifty feet from the back entrance to Frankie's.

"Good evening, Officer, find anything interesting?"

"Just these and his wallet that provided the identification of the corpse. The wallet was in one hip pocket and these were in the other." He handed him a six pack of condoms—two of which were missing. They were encased in a plastic bag to protect the evidence. "He won't be needing them anymore," he remarked as he threw the condoms into the back of the forensic van.

Forte, although accustomed to viewing homicide scenes, felt nausea rise up in him. He remembered a quote from Shakespeare, "The evil that men do lives after them. The good is oft interred with their bones." Yes, it was true. Linde would always be remembered as the priest who was shot in back of Frankie's gay bar with condoms in his pocket.

He had one more thing to do before he headed home for the night. He snapped open his cell phone and punched in the number of the archbishop's mansion. After a few rings, a voice, that he recognized as belonging to Renato Del'Ano, greeted him.

"Sorry to have to bother you again, Monsignor." No sense in beating around the bush. He came right out with it. "Monsignor Linde was murdered tonight behind Frankie's bar—shot in the head."

After a few seconds of absolute silence, Del'Ano said, "Keep me informed, Detective."

"Sure. Be very careful and tell the archbishop to

be exceedingly careful. Call me at once, if you see anything suspicious. Good night."

17

Renato

It was completely unnerving. First Zagan, then Stalker, then someone took a shot at Finolli, and now Linde had been killed behind Frankie's gay bar. How many times had Zagan told him not to go to Frankie's. Many was the time that Zagan had covered for Linde to shield him from bad publicity. He had warned him not to march in gay parades, but all to no avail. Now he was dead and the whole world knew that he was found dead behind a gay bar with condoms in his pocket with two of them missing from a six pack. The *Rosanada News* had carried the entire story on the front page and the various wire services had picked up the story and shipped it far and wide. It was only a matter of time unit Rome would phone demanding an accounting.

L'Abbadon was under almost constant sedation. He refused to leave the house to go to the chancery. What was worse he didn't want him to leave the house either. He spent his days sitting in the den holding Pigalle on his lap, petting the poodle and brushing it.

"Your Excellency," Renato said in an attempt to reason with him, "next week we have scheduled the installation of John Bugumil as auxiliary bishop. You simply have to go to the cathedral for that event. We simply can't postpone it. Many dignitaries are coming and have already made their plans. I will arrange for a police escort to take you and me to St. Mark's Cathedral and to guard the entrances and check everyone who enters. We will get them to set up metal detectors like the ones at airports and everyone will have to pass through and be checked. No guns will be brought in. You will be safe and so will I. I am just as much at risk as you are."

"All right, Renato, take care of it."

Renato phoned Detective Forte and arranged for the necessary police protection. It would not be easy, but they would take care of it. No one would be able to bring a weapon into St. Mark's.

Renato had to deal with his own fears as well as those of the archbishop. Since he was slender, small in stature and not muscular, and rather effeminate, he feared being overpowered by a large man intent on taking his life. The Beretta L'Abbadon had given him provided him with a sense of security, and he kept it always with him, prepared to kill anyone who made a move against him.

The day for John Bugumil's ordination to the episcopacy was somber with dark clouds and rain. As soon as he awakened, Renato had a feeling of impending doom and disaster. He had a difficult time waking L'Abbadon who was still drowsy from the medication he had taken to make him sleep the night before.

As the archbishop showered, he laid out his finest Italian suit, his crocodile loafers, and a stiffly starched white shirt, and his Roman collar. From the highboy dresser he fetched his underwear and socks. Everything was ready when L'Abbadon emerged from the shower in all his naked 73-yearold infamy, milk-white skin, hanging breasts, sagging buttocks, and protruding belly covering a diminutive and almost invisible cork-sized penis. Renato diverted his eyes from looking at him, knowing that he was extremely sensitive about the size of his male anatomy.

The archbishop dressed quickly as Renato handed him his clothing, item by item. When he was fully dressed, L'Abbadon shaved using his old fashioned straight razor while Renato ordered Josette to send up their breakfast in the dumb waiter in L'Abbadon's room. They still had time for coffee and a continental breakfast, before leaving for the eleven o'clock Mass of ordination at the cathedral.

"*Merde! Merde au treizième puissance!*" the archbishop exclaimed. "Get me a Band-Aid, Renato. I cut my hand on my razor."

Rushing into the bathroom where L'Abbadon stood before the lavatory, Renato grabbed a Band-Aid plaster from the medicine cabinet and put it on the bleeding cut on the archbishop's right index finger. By applying pressure on the cut, Renato managed to stop the bleeding.

"Thanks, Renato. Once I am sure the bleeding is completely stopped, I will remove the Band-Aid. I don't want to say Mass with it on my hand." Renato also noticed that L'Abbadon had nicked his face in a couple places also. His hand had become quite shaky ever since Monsignor Linde had been killed.

The drive to the cathedral was uneventful. As they drove into the center of the city with two cop cars in attendance, the wind picked up in strong gusts and the rain was pelting down. A powerful storm was obviously brewing.

As they made their way into the cathedral, Renato noticed that Detective Forte was kneeling saying the rosary in the back row of the church. He sighed deeply, relieved to see that the police were there working to protect them. No doubt Forte had a team with him.

"You have come to see the ordination?" Renato greeted him.

"Yes, I like beautiful liturgy and today is certainly an important day for Rosanada with Monsignor Bugumil being elevated to the episcopacy."

L'Abbadon nodded at Forte as they proceeded down the nave and into the sacristy where Renato would help the archbishop vest. He laid out L'Abbadon's finest chasuble of moiré imported silk with gold embroidery, as the archbishop donned a pure linen alb and tied the cincture at the waist while saying the proper prayers. He carefully removed the Band-Aid from his right hand.

After unlocking the safe, Renato removed L'Abbadon's best jeweled miter, the one that he was wearing in the painting in the living room of the archiepiscopal residence. The miter was always kept in the safe in the sacristy, because the gems were genuine emeralds, diamonds, and rubies. Renato had to admit that the old man looked seven feet tall and magnificent when he wore it, but it seemed like a great extravagance to Renato, for the archbishop had spent a small fortune on it, just to satisfy his vanity.

Renato went to fetch his pastoral staff topped with a silver crucifix like the one John Paul II always carried, while L'Abbadon reached into the drawer of the large cabinet where he kept his best purple zucchetto. "Ouch," he exclaimed. "How did that razor blade get in here? Now I got a small cut on my left hand." Renato watched as L'Abbadon found the zucchetto and took it from the drawer. When he put it on his head a strange white powder fell out of it, spilling down over his face and into his eyes, and he could not help breathing some of the dust as it choked his nostrils. With his right hand he tried to wipe the powder from his face, eyes, and from around his mouth.

"Perhaps, Your Excellency, you could go in the sacristy WC and wash it off," Renato suggested.

"No, it is nothing, Renato. I'll just brush it off," he replied picking up his jeweled miter and placing it over the zucchetto.

Renato was not prepared for what happened next. In fact, he could never have imagined the course of events that followed.

18

L'Abbadon

L'Abbadon glanced in the sacristy mirror and was pleased with what he saw. All traces of the powder in the zucchetto were gone. Because the jeweled miter made him look grand and glorious, he felt invincible, as he began the procession from the entrance of the cathedral with bishop-elect John Bugumil, Bishop Morales, Renato, and several diocesan priests that he had honored by including them as concelebrants.

As they processed down the center aisle of the nave, L'Abbadon felt a strange tingling sensation on his tongue and the inner surface of his mouth. Suddenly he began to feel light headed and weak. The muscles of his face began to twitch. Sweat was breaking out on his brow and running down his face.

By the time he had processed half way to the altar, he began to feel pain in his chest. He tried to swallow the large amounts of saliva that were forming in his mouth, but was unable to. He tried to cry out to Renato to help him, but no sound issued from his throat. His heart seemed to be beating slower and slower.

When he reached the steps to go up into the sanctuary, he could no longer stand and fell to the floor before the altar shaking with convulsions.

Renato was there bending over him, calling out for a doctor to come forward from the congregation to help the ailing prelate.

L'Abbadon was aware of the presence of the doctor, Henri Perrault, who began to examine him. Suddenly he knew Detective Forte had joined the doctor and Renato.

L'Abbadon heard Renato dismiss the congregation, asking them to disperse quietly and to pray for their archbishop who appeared to be having a heart attack. He said he would finish the mass privately in the sacristy.

L'Abbadon was conscious enough to realize that Renato, Dr. Perrault, and Detective Forte had carried him into the sacristy and placed him on the sofa there. He could hear the doctor talking to Renato and Detective Forte.

"He is experiencing bradycardia—his heart beat is very slow. We need to get him to a hospital at once."

"An ambulance has been called and is on its way," Renato told him.

"I don't think it is a heart attack. His pupils are dilated and he has depressed corneal reflexes and is suffering with dysphagia, aphonia, and paresthesia," the doctor continued.

L'Abbadon felt paralysis creeping over his body. He could not form the words with his mouth, but tried to grasp them in his mind, "O my God, I am heartily sorry..." He could not remember the rest of the prayer.

He was glad when the ambulance came and the attendants picked him up on a stretcher and began rushing him to St. Francis Hospital. He was totally unable to move by the time they got him in the emergency room. Since he was having great difficulty breathing, they inserted a tube down his throat. He could hear the doctors murmuring something about cyanosis, hypotension, and cardiac arrhythmia, as they put an IV into the back of his left hand. They drew blood and with a catheter obtained a sample of urine and sent them to the lab to be analyzed in an attempt to find out what was causing his difficulties.

Still conscious, but completely paralyzed, he was aware of being moved out of the emergency room into intensive care. Renato was with him. In a few minutes, someone came to his bed and stood staring down at him. Since his eyes were closed and he was unable to open them, he could not determine who it was. Then he recognized Renato's voice as he spoke to someone else who was present.

"Good evening, Father Dell'Anitra," Renato said.

L'Abbadon knew he was addressing the attending hospital chaplain—Father Pompeo

Dell'Anitra that he had removed from his pastorate because of unproven allegations of sexually abusing a minor.

"I am relying on you to take good care of His Excellency, Renato continued."

"Of course, you can rely on me completely, Monsignor," Pompeo replied confidently. "I will stay with him as long as he needs me."

"Before I leave, I want to anoint him and give him the last rites. I am sure you have the necessary oils and a stole. I left mine in the cathedral."

O my God, thought L'Abbadon they are getting ready to bury me.

Now Father Pompeo Dell'Anitra was talking to him.

"If you can hear me, squeeze my hand. Are you sorry for your sins?" Pompeo Dell'Anitra asked him.

He tried to squeeze the priest's hand, but his muscles would not obey him. He felt Renato anoint his head and then his hands and give him the blessing for the dying. Then he heard Renato's voice begin the rosary and Father Pompeo make the responses. When the last prayer was said, Renato left abruptly without saying goodbye.

L'Abbadon felt his life flowing from him and wanted to pray, but could not find the words or the intentions. He could hear Father Pompeo's voice speaking to him. The priest's voice became harder and harder to hear and gradually faded away. Then there was only silence and darkness...

19

Forte

The doctor in charge at the hospital who treated L'Abbadon, Dr. Harold Foster, regretted that they had been unable to do anything to save the archbishop who had died approximately two hours after having been admitted in a comatose state, unable to move or even talk.

"We will not be able to establish the cause of death until the results from the autopsy are completed. That will be several days, Detective. However, I can tell you that we do not believe that he died of natural causes. Off the record, I would hazard a guess that he was poisoned. We examined the lavage we got from his stomach and found nothing in it that would indicate food poisoning." Foster picked up his stethoscope from his desk and put it around his neck. "You will have to excuse me now, I have to see a patient."

Since there was nothing further that he could learn at St. Francis Hospital, Forte decided to pay a call on Renato Del'Ano. Perhaps he could give him some information that would be helpful. As he walked through the hospital lobby to go to his car, he saw a copy of the *Rosanada Evening News* lying on the main desk. He quickly pursued the column written by Wayne Creasy.

Archbishop L'Abbadon Dead

Archbishop Cecil Anselm L'Abbadon, suddenly taken ill at St. Mark's Cathedral this morning, as he prepared to celebrate Mass and ordain Bishop-elect John N. Bugumil, collapsed at the foot of the altar, having just entered the church in procession. He was rushed to St. Francis Hospital where doctors were unable to diagnose his strange illness. He was attended by Monsignor Renato Del'Ano and Rev. Pompeo Dell'Anitra who gave him the last rites of the Church. Funeral arrangements are pending.

Before paying Monsignor Del'Ano a call, Forte decided to stop at Mac Donald's and grab a hamburger and fries. Although it was Friday night, he did not have to hurry home, for Miguel had asked to go home from school with Jamie Shannon and he would pick him up at the Shannon home when he was finished for the evening.

When he arrived at 7 Coziness Lane in Champs De Bauchery about eight p.m., the maid, Josette d'Arras, conducted him into the living room where the Florentine candleholders were ablaze with two dozen very tall black tapers before the bigger than life portrait of the dead archbishop, creating the impression that it was a shrine to the dead man's memory. Forte studied the portrait and thought of the old phrase "*Sic transit gloria mundi.*" How different the archbishop had looked as he convulsed on the floor where he had fallen before the main altar of St. Mark's. No doubt Monsignor Del'Ano would give him a magnificent ceremony for his funeral Mass.

Del'Ano was impeccably dressed in gray linen slacks and a white sports shirt when he greeted him. Forte marveled at how self- possessed the man was. Rather small in stature with delicate features, brows that curved above almond shaped eyes, and a very serious face that evening, instead of his usual radiant Italian charm, the vicar general sat in one of the red chairs embroidered with a blazing gold dragon. Forte drew his own chair closer so that they could talk in hushed voices.

"I came to offer my condolences, Monsignor," Forte proffered as he shook the vicar general's hand. "I am sorry for your trouble."

"Thank you, Detective," Del'Ano replied in a very subdued manner. "My troubles are indeed great. I phoned the nuncio and told him of the archbishop's death. He phoned Rome and in consultation with the Head of the Congregation of Bishops has put me in charge of the archdiocese as administrator. I am probably the next target on that insane killer's hit list.

"I know what you must be going through, but I really need to ask you a few questions."

"Of course, and I do have something to tell you that might prove to be very significant. But first let me get Josette to bring us something to drink. What will it be for you, Detective? We have almost anything you would like."

"Perrier water, if you have it."

Del'Ano summoned the maid and ordered the Perrier water and scotch and soda for himself. Within minutes the beverages arrived in elegant French crystal.

"What do you have to tell me," Forte asked eagerly and willing to grasp at straws to find a solution to the gruesome murders that were keeping him awake nights, since he had no solid information that would lead him to the killer.

"This morning when we were vesting in the sacristy, something strange happened to Archbishop L'Abbadon."

Forte fixed his gaze steadily on Del'Ano waiting to hear the details. "Yes?" he said.

"When the archbishop put his zucchetto on, some white powder fell out of it onto his face, getting into his eyes and nostrils in clouds of dust. He brushed the powder away with his hands. He had cut his hand on his straight razor when he shaved this morning, because he was nervous, I guess. Since he did not want to wear it at the altar as he said

Mass, he had taken the Band-Aid off his index finger. No doubt more of the white powder got into the open wound on his finger."

"Do you have any idea what the powder was and how it got there?"

"Absolutely none. Although his Excellency had feelings of impending doom and was afraid to leave the house, we thought he would be safe in the cathedral, especially with the protection of the excellent police of Rosanada." He nodded to Forte as he said this. "It never occurred to me to tell the people in the emergency room about this. I thought he was having a heart attack."

"Where is the zucchetto now?"

"The hospital just called about forty-five minutes ago and said we could pick up the archbishop's things —pectoral cross, miter and vestments at any time."

Hearing this Forte jumped to his feet, downed the last few swallows of Perrier water, and said solemnly, "Watch out, Monsignor, be extremely careful. The killer or killers might come after you since you are now at the top of command in the archdiocese, since L'Abbadon is dead." Hastily he excused himself and hurried to the hospital to inform them of what he had just heard.

Dr. Foster had already left for the night, but he alerted a Dr. James McGivney about the powder in the zucchetto. He recovered the zucchetto from the archbishop's effects and sent it immediately to a lab to be tested to determine what the unknown white powder was.

"Let me know, Doctor, as soon as you find out anything. Could you help me locate the hospital chaplain who attended the archbishop before his death?"

"Oh, that would be Father Pompeo Dell'Anitra. A very fine priest, even if he does hold very liberal views. Although his theology is quite liberal, he has always shown great compassion in dealing with patients. He is not on duty right now. If you want to see him, he lives at Casa St. Popola's, the house the archbishop set up to house some of the members of the chancery and priests who have had allegations of pedophilia made against them. However, I really do not believe that Father Dell'Anitra is a pedophile."

Casa St. Popola, the building L'Abbadon erected to house homeless clergy including his vicar general and two of his bishops, was a modern, but very plain, apartment style building of ten suites and eight large bedrooms. The building was of Colonial design made of frame and stone with a large stone chimney. Inside, the furnishings were of exquisite taste, as was everything chosen by L'Abbadon. The furniture was Scandinavian, very plain, but highly sophisticated. Due to the extremely modern altar appointments, the private chapel appeared to have been designed by a European architect.

The dining room, where Monsignor Zagan, the vicar general, had presided at the head of the long blonde table, was solemn and impressive. In fact, the whole house spoke of the dignity of the present administration of the archdiocese, except for the atrocious paintings and prints that pretended to decorate the walls that were all painted a light cream color. The furnishings were mostly a harsh shade of yellowish green. Pretentious as it was, there was certainly none of the luxury that the archbishop built into his own residence.

Waiting in the living room for Father Dell'Anitra to come to him, Forte noticed Bishop Morales who was reading his breviary in front of the fireplace where a log was blazing. Wearing blue jeans and a plain white T-shirt, Bishop Sinew come strolling through the living room with a tall purple miter on his head. His vacant stare and bizarre attire told him that the bishop's brain tumor was taking its toll on him. He was reciting the rosary out loud much to the annoyance of Bishop Morales.

Forte spotted a priest who was sitting at a table playing solitaire and recognized him from his photos in the *Rosanada News* as the priest who was confined to St. Popola's for having confessed to abusing a ten year old child. He could not remember the man's name, but did recall that the judge had been lenient to him, because he was in his seventies and for that reason had given him three year's house arrest instead of prison.

When Father Dell'Anitra came into the living room, he was well dressed in black slacks and a black shirt. As soon as Dell'Anitra saw who was calling on him, he said, "Let's go in the alcove over there, where we can talk privately."

As soon as they were seated, Forte began his questioning. "I'm sorry to disturb you, Father, but you attended the archbishop when he died. Is that correct?"

"Yes, I will be happy to answer your questions. What would you like to know?" Forte was glad that the priest seemed so well disposed to talking with him.

"Tell me what happened."

"When I saw the patient, Monsignor Del'Ano was with him. We gave him the last rights. L'Abbadon could not talk and so was unable to make his confession, but Monsignor Del'Ano anointed him. He could not even squeeze our hands to let us know he was conscious. We said the rosary together, Monsignor and I."

"Then what?"

"Monsignor left and I remained with the dying archbishop until he was pronounced dead. He died a violent death—twisting and turning in agony, gasping for breath." The priest was very matter of fact as he recounted the details of L'Abbadon's death.

"Did he regain consciousness before the end? Did he say anything?"

"No, to both questions. He just died with a whimper. It is had to believe that the great man is dead and that he died such a horrible death. Do you suppose he was murdered like the others in the chancery? Who would want to kill him?

"That is what I intend to find out."

When he arrived at the Shannon home to pick up Jamie about nine o'clock, the boys were busy in the kitchen making popcorn, while Mrs. Shannon was solicitously fluttering about seeing that everything was under control. He was glad his son had friends whom he could trust to look after the boy. However, his opinion of the Shannons was about to change.

20

Renato

Fear clutched at Renato, a dull aching terror that dogged his heals no matter where he went. Every sound, every unexpected noise startled him. Every footstep he imagined to be a threat to his life. He lay awake in bed every night until about four in the morning, with his Baretta under his pillow. Only with the approaching dawn did he deem it safe to fall asleep. Awakening about ten, he showered, shaved, dressed, ate a quick breakfast, and headed for the chancery to take care of business.

Although he had not yet been consecrated a bishop because of L'Abbadon's murder, John Bugumil had moved into Stalker's office and was very efficient at getting things done. He seemed quite grieved at L'Abbadon's death, probably because he had known him well, having worked as his secretary and having lived with him in the archiepiscopal residence.

A pall lay over the entire chancery. Msgr. Rattlet, the treasurer who was rumored to be a very discrete womanizer, called in sick and refused to come into the chancery. Neither he nor Msgr. Toccafondi, who always had a scheme for bringing in more funds to the archdiocese, even came to view L'Abbadon as he lay in state before the high altar of St. Mark's.

The responsibility for everything fell on Renato. He sent out invitations far and wide for members of the hierarchy to attend. Few chose to come, in view of the circumstances of the archbishop's death and the murders of the former vicar general, the chancellor, and the promoter of justice. Even the papal nuncio sent his regrets.

Wearing his jeweled miter and finest vestments, L'Abbadon lay in state in an empty cathedral with only a few policemen to guard him. Renato realized that the members of the clergy were too terrified even to stop to pay their respects. A few lay people drifted in and out, pausing for a few moments to pray before the catafalque that was surrounded by a row of tall white candles that were to burn continually until the funeral Mass.

Renato asked Bishop-elect John Bugumil and Bishop Morales to concelebrate the funeral Mass with him. The bishop-elect was an outgoing, jovial, and usually happy-go-lucky traditionalist who served L'Abbadon well, for the archbishop had bestowed upon him, in a short time, a variety of ecclesiastical titles and dignities that are usually accorded to older priests. Now he was selected to be an auxiliary bishop. As the three of them began the Mass in the almost deserted cathedral with only the immediate family of L'Abbadon and the ever present old ladies who never missed a funeral Mass, Bugumil's gentle hazel eyes looked very sad. Together they laid L'Abbadon to rest in a crypt next to Zagan, whose killer was still running loose, striking fear into the hearts of the priests of the chancery.

Even though Rosanada police were always present in the chancery building, Renato, who now had the office in which Zagan had been murdered, kept his door locked and bolted. Although the blood stains had been cleaned from the carpet, an atmosphere of death clung to the room. Despite the fact that Brinks had installed a new security system in the chancery that he insisted be constantly armed, that did not present a problem, because very, very few people had business that would bring them into the chancery, preferring to do all their communicating by phone, fax, or email.

Feelings of terror stabbed at his heart, as he sat at Zagan's former desk with his Baretta in the inside breast pocket of his suit.

21

Jamie Shannon

Father Minimo was wonderful! Jamie was learning a lot from him almost every afternoon after school, when he met him at St. Dymphna's. The church was closed; the altar was stripped and so was the sacristy. Jamie missed seeing all the candles burning in front of the statue of St. Dymphna with the demon on a chain. Sometimes it seemed to Jamie as if the demon came alive for his red eyes appeared to be staring at him, watching him in whatever direction he moved in the old church. The blue, red, and green glass windows did not let in very much light, and so the shadows looked like crouching lions ready to pounce on him.

Although the church had been closed by the archbishop, Father Minimo had kept a key to the sacristy door and made a copy of it and gave it to him so he could slip in quietly and unobserved, for the sacristy was on the rear of the building and the adjoining lots behind the church were vacant. It made him feel important and like a priest to have a key to the sacristy just like Father Minimo.

He had arrived a little early that afternoon, but knew that Father Minimo would soon be there and today he was bringing with him his friend Gautier. He liked Gautier who was only a few months older than he and always had fun things to do and talk about. Gautier had told him that he was a voodoo priest, but Jamie did not know exactly what that meant, but if it was OK with Father Minimo, it was OK with him.

It was almost five o'clock and night was beginning to fall when he glanced out the sacristy door to see if he could spot Father Minimo and Gautier approaching. The wind had picked up and autumn leaves were swirling around the sacristy door, for it was October and soon it would be Halloween. He always liked Halloween and dressing up like a ghost or goblin and haunting the neighborhood for handouts of candy and cookies. This year was going to be different. Father Minimo said they would do something very special right there in St. Dymphna's and he would be a part of it. They were going to have a big celebration.

The wind blew a branch of a tree against the sacristy window and the screeching sound that it made frightened him. He slammed the sacristy door shut and looked around, hoping he could find a candle, so he would not have to wait in the darkness.

Thinking that he might possibly find a candle on the candle stand in front of the statue of St. Sebastian, he headed slowly toward the back of the church. He fumbled in the darkness and found a large votive candle lying unused in the very back of the candle rack. There was even a match. Just when the candle began to burn, he heard Father Minimo and Gautier open the sacristy door and then come into the church, bringing with them a battery operated lantern.

"Sorry we are late, Jamie. We had to stop to buy some things for our Halloween celebration. Look at the nice black candles we found." He stuck them in a box and put them away in a cabinet in the sacristy where he said no one would find them.

"I never saw black candles before. It *must* be a special celebration if we are going to use black candles," Jamie said filled with wonder.

"See what else we got," Gautier said, as he pulled something shiny and silver from a brown paper bag.

"What is that?" Jamie asked as he examined the five pointed object.

"That is a pentagram," explained Minimo. "It is a special symbol.

"What does it do?"

"You will have to wait 'til Halloween to see." Minimo said mysteriously.

"What are we going to do?" asked Jamie trying to coax some of the details of the celebration from Father Minimo or Gautier.

"Don't look at me," exclaimed Gautier denying any knowledge of what Minimo was planning.

"Come, sit down on this chair here in the

sanctuary, and I will tell you a little bit about it, but it is our super secret, you know, you can't tell anyone. Understand?"

"OK, you can trust me."

"We are going to celebrate a Black Mass Halloween night right here. It is an old Halloween tradition."

Jamie became wide-eyed with enthusiasm. "Cool!" he exclaimed. "Will I get to take part in the ritual?"

"Of course, you are going to be a very important part of it. We are going to initiate you—a secret initiation—into our fellowship."

"That sounds really cool!" Eager to learn what to expect, he asked "What do I have to do?"

"Yeah," said Gautier "What do I have to do?"

"Gautier, you will play your voodoo drums so everyone can dance to the music."

"*Bon*! said Gautier reverting to his Haitian French patois. "How many people do you think will come?" The light from the lantern cast strange shadows on Gautier's face, making him look fierce. His eyes were dark and penetrating as he waited for Minimo to explain.

"Twenty or thirty, I have asked all my friends from Frankie's bar to come and my friend Father Pompeo. I did not tell him what we planned to do. I wanted to surprise him," Minimo explained as he rose from the chair and began walking around the sanctuary, apparently assessing the place for its

Josué Raúl Conte

suitability for his planned activities.

"What do I do, Father Minimo?" Jamie asked as he twisted impatiently on the chair formerly reserved for an altar boy.

"You will be the altar. I bought a special stoneware cup and plate for the occasion." He opened a brown bag that he had placed on the floor next to his chair, where he had sat in the past to preside in St. Dymphna's on Saturday nights when he said Mass.

Jamie looked at Minimo with bewilderment. "I don't understand."

"It is simple. You get down on your hands and knees here in the sanctuary in front of the altar. Here I will show you."

Clumsily Minimo, holding on to a chair, lowered his large muscular frame to the floor and went down on his hands and knees. "Look, it is important to keep your back straight like an altar. Like this. Now do you understand?"

"Why am I going to be the altar? Why isn't Gautier going to be it instead of me?"

"Because you are the one who is going to be initiated. You said you wanted to learn about being a priest, didn't you. Gautier has already been initiated; besides he is going to play his drums." Awkwardly Minimo pulled himself to a standing position. Pointing at the floor in front of the abandoned altar of the deserted church, he said, "Now Jamie, you try it." He motioned for him to drop to the floor.

157

When Jamie had assumed the proper position, Minimo bent over him and ran his hands up and down the boy's back and patted him on the rump, letting his hand linger over the boy's posterior while his fingers seemed to be caressing him."

"You are doing great, kid." Minimo said with enthusiasm, taking the boy by the arm and helping him to his feet.

"You will make a great altar," Gautier joined in as he reached over and patted him on the rear.

"Now, you better run on along home," Minimo advised. "We don't want to worry your mother by having you come home late."

When he arrived home, his mother and brother were already there and dinner was in the oven. How much he wished he could tell them about the wonderful thing that was going to happen on Halloween when he would be initiated at the Black Mass. He couldn't understand why he had to keep something so special a secret.

22

Forte

The results for the autopsy of L'Abbadon revealed that he had been killed by a compound of various things, some of which they could not identify, but the main poison and the one responsible for the dramatic collapse and death of the archbishop was a neurotoxin obtained from the puffer fish and one of the deadliest known to science. The toxin is called tetrodotoxin, or more exactly anhydrotetrodotoxin 4-epitetrodotoxin and is about 1200 times deadlier than cyanide. There were also traces of poison taken from a sea frog present in the body. How anyone in Rosanada could have obtained these things was a great mystery to him. Perhaps if he could figure that out, he would have a lead that would take him to the killer or killers. How they had used the poison to kill L'Abbadon was ingenious. Obviously it had to be someone who had access to the sacristy of St. Mark's Cathedral and someone who hated L'Abbadon enough to go to extremes to get rid of him. Although chalices, patens, ciboriums, monstrances, the jeweled miter and the crosier of the archbishop were kept under lock and key in the sacristy, the closet for the vestments and the drawers for zucchettos, stoles, and altar linens were not. The killer could have slipped unnoticed into the sacristy and planted the poison during the hours the cathedral was open to the public.

What a relief it would be to catch the killer or killers responsible for all the chancery murders. He needed more free time to spend with Miguel and time to persuade Anita to return home. Her main complaint had always been that he was working on a case, night after night, when she wanted him to be at home. Now almost every night recently he was required to work. When he did go home, the empty house filled him with pain. Everything in the house spoke to him of Anita. She had done a beautiful job of making the house into a real home. The lovely ruffled lace curtains that she made to decorate the windows, the cozy slipcovers she created for the living room, the African violets growing on the window sill in the kitchen—all these things symbolized her and made him ache for her to return. With a very heavy heart he undressed, took a shower, and jumped into the king-sized bed that he had shared with her for nineteen years, but sleep evaded him. He heard the clock in the living room chime two, before he finally drifted off to a troubled sleep.

Dreams of darkness and horror made him toss

and turn. Someone was trying to hurt Miguel. A dark shadowy figure was holding his son hostage in a strange and desolate place as he tried to find where he was. When he finally discovered where the dark figure was holding Miguel, he rushed there determined to arrive before it was too late.

Just as he was drawing near to the abandoned building, an explosion occurred, completely destroying it and Miguel. In a cold sweat, he awoke suddenly with terror and panic overwhelming him. "Thank God, it was only a dream!" he exclaimed as he made his way to the refrigerator in the kitchen where he poured himself a glass of milk, before returning to his bed.

When he awakened in the morning all memory of the dream had vanished, but he harbored a sense of dread, a feeling that something was terribly wrong. It was Friday morning and it was Halloween. No doubt that evening there would be the usual Halloween tricks with kids soaping windows and ringing doorbells asking for treats.

"Today is Halloween, Dad," Miguel said with enthusiasm bubbling in his voice as he ate his breakfast cereal.

"Yeah, I know. I used to have a lot of fun on Halloween myself when I was your age. They say it has become one of the biggest holidays of the year. Have you got a costume?"

"I have got a mask of the devil with horns on it. I am going to wear some black slacks and a black jacket."

"Well, I am sorry I cannot be here with you tonight. Perhaps you can go home with Jamie Shannon again?"

"That is what I figured, so we already made plans for tonight for me to be with him."

"Well, I will try to get done early. Take your cell phone with you and I will phone you and let you know when I am ready to pick you up."

Forte dropped Miguel off at Santiago parish High School and drove off before he realized that the boy had forgotten his cell phone and had left it on the seat of the car.

All day long, feelings of impending disaster and dread assailed him, as he continued visiting and interviewing everyone that he felt could possibly give him information about the chancery murders. Late morning, he gave Anita a call.

"Let's have lunch together today at one. I would like to talk to you about Miguel," he invited.

Before answering, she hesitated. "Please, God, don't let her say 'no.'" he prayed, holding his breath hoping she would agree to meet him.

"All right," she replied. "Where shall we meet?"

"Anywhere you like," he answered willing to go out of his way to please her.

"Make it the Skytop at the Hyatt Regency. Their lunch buffet is the best in the city."

When he arrived at the Skytop at exactly one, Anita was already there seated at a table that had a beautiful view of the Rosanada River valley that was ablaze with the colors of autumn. The maple trees were a bright orange red and the oaks a deep burnished Cordovan leather brown. It was a glorious day with a cerulean blue sky that made one feel great just to be alive.

Now that he was with Anita again, his spirits lifted and he noticed her soft feminine dress that was a gentle shade of green that complimented the color of her eyes. Her warm golden skin tones were radiant as she sat there in the autumn sunshine, when he approached and took a seat opposite her. "You look lovely. Beautiful dress," he said.

"I came here today," she spoke softly, "so that we could talk about Miguel." She took a sip of water and unfolded her napkin.

"Of course. Let's first get our food from the buffet," he suggested, rising and helping her with her chair.

They proceeded to the buffet where the chef was slicing prime rib of beef—always his favorite. Modestly selecting food for his plate that would not cause him to gain weight, he chose the beef, salads, and vegetables. Anita was always neat and trim and had grown only more beautiful with the passing of the years. Everyone had always said they were a handsome couple—she with her patrician good looks and he with his tall muscular masculine build.

Once they had returned to their table, Anita commented, "Miguel tells me that you have been letting him go home with Jamie Shannon after school on Fridays. Is that correct?" She spread a biscuit with the herb flavored butter that the Skytop was famous for and waited for him to answer, before taking a bite of it.

"Yes, that is true. The Shannons seem to be fine people. They go to our church. Jamie and Joey are fine boys. I hear Jamie wants to be a priest when he grows up."

"Well, I certainly hope Miguel doesn't get any ideas like that. You told me of your experience in the seminary. I certainly would not want him to go to a seminary. Especially now with all the murders that have been taking place in the archdiocese lately." She picked delicately at her salad. "Do you think it is a good idea for him to go to the Shannons?"

"Well, if you just came back home to us…"

"Not much point in that. You are working almost every night. What kind of life is that for me and for you and for Miguel? Do I make my point clear? I don't like having him go home with the Shannons. If fact, I am very much opposed to it."

"OK, I will try to finish early this evening and pick him up earlier than usual. I do want to accommodate you and do everything I can to please you. Just give me some time, and I will find a way to stop working nights. If I am home every night, will you be there too?" He looked at her with apprehension written on his rugged but handsome features.

"We will see. That would be a step in the right direction. I will tell you this. I will not return to you until, and unless, you do stop all the night work. I will, however, not promise you anything."

A glimmer of hope seemed to break on the horizon of his heart. They shook hands and parted friends, if not lovers.

Determined to keep his word that he would pick up Miguel early from the Shannons, he gave Mrs. Shannon a call about seven thirty.

"Good evening, Mrs. Shannon, Detective Forte here. I'm calling to let you know that I am ready to come for Miguel now. Would you have him get ready?"

"They boys aren't here right now. Jamie and Miguel went out for a while. I am sure they will be back before long."

"Well, can you tell me where they went? I will go there and find him."

"Let's see. Oh, yes, Jamie said they were going to trick or treat on the way to St. Dymphna's."

"But wasn't St. Dymphna's one of the parishes that was shut down by the archdiocese?"

"Yes, but they are going to meet that nice Father Tabron there this evening. He has a key and they are having Halloween festivities there tonight. He always has that nice young man Gautier from Haiti with him."

"Thank you." He hung up the phone. An alarm

went off in his head! Something was terribly wrong! Tabron was one of the priests that had been removed from his parish because of sexual allegations having been levied against him. He had to get there before it was too late, but he needed back up. He could not do it alone.

23

Pompeo

Minimo had been very insistent. Otherwise he would not have gone to St. Dymphna's to see the Halloween events that he had planned there. Although he certainly was not enthusiastic about going, he left St. Popola's shortly after dinner and drove through the bright moonlit night to the old church where Minimo used to say Mass on Saturdays until it was permanently closed. As he drove through the streets of Rosanada, he saw many groups of kids dressed as goblins, ghosts, and demons rushing through the night, yelling "Trick or treat!" Surely, he thought, Minimo is beyond such things.

When he arrived at St. Dymphna's, he was surprised to see that a large number of cars were parked near the deserted church. Only the slightest amount of light shone from the red, blue, and green glass windows. One had to look twice to even notice it.

As he made his way up the weather-beaten and warped steps at the front of the church, he recognized Monsignor Finolli coming up the sidewalk, heading for the church building. Not wanting to be recognized, he waited for Finolli to enter the church ahead of him. Once inside the church, he noticed that the holy water fonts were filled with sand. A few candles in red votive glasses burned before the statue of St. Sebastian. In the dim light, the martyred saint seemed to come alive with his gaping wounds crying out for mercy. The arrows that stuck in his flesh actually seemed to quiver in the half light of the flickering candles.

In amazement, he glanced around the church, noting that at least twenty people were already assembled in the pews. He recognized them as being some of the same people he had seen at Frankie's bar. In fact, he spotted the young man that Finolli had been dancing with at Frankie's, as well as a few other priests, including, of all people, Monsignor Billy King. While Minimo and Gautier, his protégé, were busy in the sanctuary getting ready for the evening events, he noted that some of the Haitians he had seen in Gautier's peristyle were seated together in the front pews.

Utterly grotesque was the statue of St. Dymphna holding her severed head onto the bleeding stump that was her neck. The demon that she held fast by a chain in her hand seemed to be pulling on the chain in an attempt to be set free. The red stones in his eye sockets glowed in the dark, giving him the appearance of being alive.

On the altar of the abandoned church were two candle holders, bearing tall black candles that Gautier was lighting with a match that burned his fingers, causing him to wince with pain. He was wearing the red saclike garment that he had worn the night Pompeo had seen him sacrifice the chicken and drink its hot blood, before calling down the spirits. Pompeo watched as Gautier placed a large silver emblem on the altar between the candles. It looked like an inverted star and resembled the head of a goat with horns held high. He recognized that it was a pentagram—the symbol of the demonic. Next he supposed Minimo would appear in a Halloween costume dressed up like the devil. Little did it matter to him, for he simply did not believe in anything demonic. It was ridiculous to believe in Satan and hell—a carry over from the Dark Ages when men's minds were less sophisticated.

To his amazement Minimo approached the altar dressed all in black—a black chasuble and a black alb, carrying a large crucifix that he placed on the altar upside down. There was no doubt in his mind now that Minimo was once again lost in schizophrenia.

Intrigued as to what Minimo was up to, Pompeo watched as Gautier led a boy in front of the altar where the black tapers were now burning brightly in the darkness of the sanctuary. The youth, naked except for a black sheet that covered his young body, was apparently heavily sedated and drugged.

Submissively, he followed the Haitian's directions and fell to the floor on his hands and knees over a bench that supported him.

When Minimo took a thurible in hand and began incensing the altar that bore the candles and then the body of the boy, Gautier began beating a voodoo drum softly at first and then with increasing fervor until the sound came to a crescendo as clouds of smoke filled the sanctuary. The stench that greeted his nostrils told Pompeo that Minimo was burning sulfur in his censor. It was then that he realized that Minimo was going to celebrate a *Missa Niger*—a Black Mass—using the body of the youth as his altar.

No longer surprised by anything Minimo might do, Pompeo just sat there in the very dark abandoned church where the few candles that were burning cast grotesque shadows that looked like demons. In the very faint light, he could see that there were bats hanging from the rafters. Occasionally one of them would break loose and fly wildly around the black candles that were burning in the sanctuary. As Minimo began saying the Lord's Prayer backwards, a large toad hopped across the sanctuary. Pompeo had to admit that Minimo *was* putting on a good show. He settled back in his pew determined to see just what his friend would do. Nothing could possibly surprise him. Nor did he care that Minimo was preparing to celebrate a Black Mass. He had ceased to believe in the Eucharist a long time ago.

Solemnly Minimo placed an earthenware chalice and a bowl on the back of the young man who served as an altar. Rebel and renegade priests who had lost their faith had always celebrated Black Masses on the naked body of a virgin who was violated during the rituals. Remembering that Minimo had been accused of sexually abusing a young male, Pompeo realized that pedophiles would not use a female virgin, but rather a young male.

As though hypnotized, Pompeo kept watching the proceedings. After leading his strange congregation—they were all dressed completely in black—in a litany to all the demons of hell, Minimo removed the black cloth that covered the handsome naked body of the youth who remained motionless. Obviously he had been drugged to such a degree that he was oblivious to what was taking place. Pompeo watched as Minimo placed the earthenware chalice and bowl on the boy's back. Then he took something that resembled a small black triangular wafer and placed it on a dish beside the chalice.

The men seated around Pompeo were clapping their hands to the beat of the voodoo drums and calling out to Minimo urging him on.

"Go ahead!" some yelled. "Do it, man!"

"*Allez-y!*" shouted the Haitians. While he appeared to be almost in a hypnotic state, Minimo responded to the congregation by lifting up his chasuble and unzipping his fly and proceeding to urinate in the earthenware chalice.

The men in the pews—there were no women present—cheered as Minimo prepared his offering of the black triangle and the chalice of urine to the demonic powers. As Minimo sprinkled some of the contents of the chalice on his naked body, the boy was completely motionless. Nor did he stir when Minimo pushed the back triangle up the boy's rectum.

"*Allez-y! allez-y!*" cried the Haitians still louder than before. Now they were standing in the front pew, stamping their feet keeping time with the beating of the voodoo drums. Pompeo saw Monsignor Finolli clapping his hands with gusto, seeming to enjoy the ritual intensely. Father Billy

J. King, standing right behind Finolli, was equally entranced. Dropping his cane down onto the bench of the pew, he hobbled to the center aisle, and then began dancing, his limp forgotten as he swayed sensuously to and fro to the music of the voodoo drums. Immediately he was joined by many others who threw off all restraint and danced wildly up and down the center aisle.

"Let's get on with it!" yelled one of the dancing men. When Minimo gave the signal, the men in the aisle, followed by those still in the pews ran down the center aisle and began dancing around the naked boy who was oblivious to their presence. He appeared to be completely sedated by some powerful drug. Pompeo who remained hidden in the shadows in the back of the church was horrified when Minimo brutally began sodomizing him. As soon as Minimo withdrew, Monsignor Finolli quickly had his turn at raping him. Then one after another the Haitians and the other men present took turns sodomizing the boy. Horrified Pompeo watched as blood began dripping from the boy's mutilated body. He could watch no more—he had to get out of there as fast as he could. He bounded down the aisle, but when he heard the wailing of a siren, he hid in the shadows of the vestibule.

The howling of the siren subsided when a police car came rushing up to St. Dymphna's and stopped with squealing brakes. Peaking out the door, Pompeo saw Detective Forte jump from the car and come running with his pistol in hand up the steps of the church. A second police car arrived and four officers joined Forte as he entered St. Dymphna's. Pompeo kept hidden in a dark corner of the vestibule where he could see everything that was taking place and no one would find him.

24

Forte

Pandemonium broke loose in the dark and dismal church. In an attempt to hide their crimes, Gautier lifted up the boy who had been sodomized and dragged him by the wrists into the sacristy. As the police officers, with guns in hand, raced through the church, most of those present escaped through the back doors. In desperation Forte ran up to the sanctuary, shouting "Miguel! Miguel!"

One of the police officers put handcuffs and leg shackles on Minimo and put him in the squad car. Another officer did the same with Gautier.

"Miguel! Miguel! Where are you," Forte yelled in desperation.

Entering the sanctuary, he saw the bleeding naked body of a boy lying in a corner on the floor. "Miguel!" he cried. When he shined his flashlight on the face of the youth, he saw that was not his son, but Jamie Shannon. Immediately he summoned an ambulance to take Jamie to the hospital.

"Miguel!" he called. There was no response to his cries. He ransacked the sacristy trying to find some clue that would lead him to his son. He finally found him in the back of a closet behind closed doors.

"Get up, Son. It's your dad! You are safe now." The boy did not rouse. He had been drugged and apparently was totally unaware of his father's presence and the horrors of Minimo's Halloween celebration. Swiftly he picked him up and carried him to his car. He would take him to St. Francis Hospital and have him treated for drug intoxication.

Minimo Tabron and Gautier, his Haitian friend, would pay for what they had done. He would see to that. He knew that Haitians dabbled in strange exotic poisons, and he felt sure in his gut that he had found L'Abbadon's killers. He only hoped that they had not used the same poison on Jamie Shannon and Miguel that they had used on L'Abbadon.

With the siren of his squad car screaming as loud as it would go, Cristian Forte rushed through the streets of Rosanada to St. Francis Hospital with Miguel who was still unconscious.

"Please, God," he prayed, "give me back my son. Reunite our family."

When Anita found out what had happened to their son and Jamie Shannon, she would be furious with him. How could he ever hope to get her to come back home now?

He phoned Mrs. Shannon, breaking to her the bad news of what had happened to Jamie, advising her to go at once to the hospital to be with her son.

In the emergency room at St. Francis, the

doctors were working hard to save Miguel. They pumped his stomach, hoping to rid him of the drugs that had rendered him lifeless and comatose. They took samples of his blood and with a catheter a sample of his urine to be tested to learn what it was that had been given to him. Then they put Miguel in intensive care.

He knew what he had to do. On his cell phone he called Anita.

"Something has happened to Miguel. I think he is going to be all right. He is in St. Francis hospital. The doctors are working on him now. Perhaps you should come over here and be with him."

The doctors allowed him to sit in a solemn vigil at the bedside of his son. His boyish body looked very small as he lay there still and lifeless with an IV hooked up to his left hand. When Forte brushed his brown curly hair back off his forehead, he felt cold to the touch. His breathing was labored and his pulse rapid. Although his eyelids fluttered from time to time, the boy did not open his eyes.

Anita arrived within minutes of his call. Frantic that something had happened to her child, she blamed Forte. "I told you he never should have been allowed to go home with the Shannons. I'll never forgive you for this!" She stared at him, haggard and weary under the fluorescent lights of the hospital and no longer the beautiful bride he had married nineteen years before.

"I'm sorry!" he pleaded. "I would never do

anything to hurt either of you. Please forgive me!"

She turned her back on him and walked to the other side of Miguel's bed, where she sat down beside their son. Taking his hand in hers, she began speaking to Miguel.

"Mama is here, Miguel. Wake up, please wake up," she pleaded.

The boy stirred ever so slightly.

"Nurse," Forte called, "Nurse, come here, he is waking up."

The nurse, a very professional middle-aged black woman, came into the alcove where they were and began taking Miguel's vital signs. "His blood pressure is getting back to normal," she announced authoritatively. "I think that pumping his stomach helped a lot. He was drugged, but the dose was not lethal." She listened to his heart and added, "His pulse is almost normal now. I think he will come out of this stupor soon. He is a strong young man and is making a good come back."

A half hour later, Miguel open his dark brown eyes and looked up into the face of his mother who was caressing his forehead with her finger tips. "Thank God!" she exclaimed.

"Yes, thank God," Forte agreed.

As soon as it was apparent that the boy would fully recover, the nurse had him moved into a private room. Anita made arrangements to spend the night on a roll-away set up next to his bed.

To say good night, Forte took the boy's hands in

his and smiled at him warmly. "Tomorrow is Saturday, Miguel. We will make it a very special day, I will pick you up as soon as you are discharged— the nurse told me you would be free to go about eleven in the morning after the doctor makes his rounds. I will spend the entire day with you and we will do whatever you want. Promise!" With a faint and weak smile, Miguel looked up at him and said, "Great, Dad!"

"No!," Anita protested, taking her son in her arms. "Miguel will not spend the weekend with you, Cristian." Her face was flushed with anger. "I will pick him up and take him home with me. I simply cannot trust you with him anymore."

He saw that it was useless trying to argue with her. To avoid further conflict, he reached down and ruffled Miguel's hair and said, "Good night, Son."

And then addressing Anita, he told her, "Good night, Anita. I am truly sorry this has happened."

Refusing to acknowledge he had spoken to her, she turned her back on him, ignoring him completely. Disconsolate, he turned sadly and silently left Miguel's room.

Before leaving the hospital, he inquired about Jamie Shannon and was directed to his bedside in intensive care. The doctors had finished treating him. They had given him an enema, washed out his rectum thoroughly, cleansing him of massive amounts of semen, gave him antibiotics, and sewed up all the places that had been torn open by the forceful entry of so many violators. He had been heavily drugged, but no permanent damage had been done. He would recover completely.

Seeing that the boy was awake, he bent over him, took his hand in his, and said, "I will make them pay for what they have done to you, Jamie." The boy's eyelids fluttered. Timidly he glanced up at Forte.

"Thank you for saving me and bringing me here."

"I know you must be having a lot of pain, Jamie."

The boy's eyes were sad and tormented, as he replied," Yes, Sir, I am. My body hurts, but my soul hurts much more. I wanted to be a priest. They told me that they would initiate me so I could become one of them. Why did God let this happen to me?"

"That is a question people have been asking ever since Adam and Eve encountered the serpent in the garden," he replied. "I don't know all the answers, Jamie, but I can tell you this. God always brings great good from evil. The greater the evil, the greater the good that God can derive from it. What can be worse than killing Jesus?"

"I can't think of anything worse than that," Jamie replied trying to follow what he was saying.

"No, there is nothing worse than trying to kill God. You do believe that Jesus is God, don't you?"

"Yes, I do."

"Well, because evil men killed Jesus, God brought tremendous good from that. Because he was crucified, Jesus rose from the dead to save mankind from death and destruction. Because he was crucified, Jesus is able to give eternal life to those who believe in Him, love Him, and keep His commandments. To live in God forever is the greatest good that man can receive from God. And we would not have that gift, if evil men had not killed Jesus."

"But what has that got to do with what happened to me last night?" Jamie protested biting his lower lip. His deep brown eyes were filled with doubt and despair.

"Throughout life, you will encounter evil. You will try to be on the look out for it and to avoid it, but evil will eventually come to you many times in your lifetime. It is up to you how you deal with it. You can let it make you bitter and mean, or you can accept it and let it make you grow in unconditional love. We must always forgive those who hurt us and despitefully use us. We must forgive like Jesus forgives. If we do that, we will learn to love the way Jesus loves—unconditionally. The only thing that will bring you happiness in this world is unconditional love. If you learn to love unconditionally, you will be like Jesus. And someday, you might even become His priest. The Church will change. There are a lot of priests like Minimo, but there also a lot of really dedicated holy men of God in the priesthood. Our Church is not just for today. We have a two thousand year tradition with glorious saints of God to inspire us and encourage us. We are the Church of the Apostle Paul, St. Augustine, St, Francis, St. Ignatius, and countless others who have been transformed by the Holy Spirit into great saints. We are also the Church of the future. All God asks of us is to let the Holy Spirit mold us and form Christ in us and make us a glorious Church. The future is up to us and God. Forget what has happened to you tonight, and let God heal you and lead you. Forget Minimo and the others and let God make you into a true priest of Jesus Christ."

A flicker of hope shone in Jamie's eyes. "Is it possible? Could it really happen to me? Now I feel dirty and abused—violated." He lowered his eyes, as if consumed by shame.

"You have done nothing to be ashamed of. I'm proud of you and the way you have survived this ordeal. When the time comes for you to go to the seminary, and if you still want to be a priest, I promise you I will find a seminary for you where the gospel is still taught and believed—a place where holy men shepherd those who want to follow Jesus and serve him in the priesthood." His words were comforting the boy who was beginning to relax and even smile faintly.

Forte sat then in silence by the boy's bed until he got drowsy and fell asleep. On his way out, the nurse at the desk told him that Mrs. Shannon had visited Jamie earlier, but had to leave to return home to her other son who was alone in their house.

Because he had unfinished business and could not go .home yet, he drove to police headquarters where Minimo and Gautier were being held. Since he was the arresting officer, he wanted to charge them as quickly as he could. He also needed a court order to search Minimo's and Gautier's apartments, which he would do the next day. He felt sure he would find the neurotoxin poison that killed L'Abbadon and connect them to his death. As he drove home to his empty house he was convinced that the case was about to crack wide open. However, something very unusual and totally unexpected occurred.

25

Forte

Early the next morning, Forte got the search warrant and, even though it was his day off, went to the apartments of Minimo and Gautier to look for the poison that killed L'Abbadon. After searching Minimo's apartment thoroughly, he decided that there was nothing there to tie him to any of the murders. That did not mean the man was innocent, however, but just meticulous and careful.

In Gautier's apartment, he had more success. Never before in his life had he ever seen anything like Gautier's apartment. Very little was to be seen in the living room, which had been turned into some sort of place to hold religious services. Cushions were scattered around a pole in the middle of the room. In an adjoining room, he spotted an altar with statues of strange looking people. He found what he was looking for on a table in the rear of the room—green and blue bottles marked with skull and cross bones and some plain red bottles. Just as he ordered the men of his crew to gather up all the bottles carefully and take them to their van, a strange man came out of an adjoining bedroom and approached him.

"Good day, I have a court order to search this place," he told the man emphatically.

The man, a big, black-skinned Haitian, came shuffling closer to him, but said not a world. His eyes were vacant as if there were no one at home in his head. Mechanically the man lumbered across the room with his arms hanging lifelessly at his sides. Forte had never seen a zombie, but he figured that if they really exist, he had encountered one. The man was apparently totally mute and incapable of any kind of communication or interaction. Strangely he reached down and picked up a big black tomcat that was rubbing its head on his legs. The cat had the same vacant stare in its eyes as did the man. Remembering how Jamie Shannon and his own son had been immobilized the night before with drugs, he concluded that the man had also suffered from the administration of some unknown substance that rendered him almost lifeless. Perhaps the contents of the bottles he had sequestered would explain his condition as well as show what had killed L'Abbadon and immobilized his son and Jamie Shannon.

After ordering his crew to take the confiscated bottles immediately to homicide to have them analyzed, he went to interview Minimo and Gautier.

The two men had been kept separate ever since he had booked them the night before. Now he would interview them separately and then look for discrepancies in their stories. First he would see Minimo who was brought to him at once.

"I demand to see my attorney," Minimo Tabron yelled at him, as soon as he had entered his office. "I am innocent. Well, we did play around with the Shannon kid a bit, but I am not guilty of murder. We just gave the kid something to drug him, but would not hurt him permanently." Tabron was haggard from the sleepless night he had spent in the lockup.

"Where were you when L'Abbadon was killed?"

"I was in the cathedral watching him process down the aisle, and that is all I will tell you until my lawyer is here."

"Take him away," Forte snapped to the guard who had brought Tabron to him. "And bring me the other one."

Almost at once the guard brought Gautier d'Arras into his office. He was wearing a very sullen expression as Forte confronted him, asking where he was when L'Abbadon was murdered. The scar that reached from the corner of his eye down to his mouth was livid as the Haitian became furious that he had been arrested and suspected of murder. "I have nothing to say," he mumbled and his face became stony as he refused to talk.

When the lab report came back on the contents of the bottles in Gautier's apartment, it confirmed Forte's suspicions. One of the bottles contained the neurotoxin that had killed the archbishop. The sample was identical to the one taken from L' Abbadon's zucchetto. In another bottle they found the drug that had been used on Jamie Shannon and Miguel. Laboratory anaylsis confirmed that it was a preparation that would have no lasting effect on the boys.

In addition to the puffer fish toxin there was also contained in the blue bottles poison from the sea frog and from a species of snake that was commonly found in Haiti. There was no doubt in his mind that he had found the murderers of L'Abbadon, Zagan, Stalker, and Linde. Now all he needed to do was find the gun that had killed Linde and see if any of the fingerprints on the brass cigar lighter that killed Stalker were Tabron's or those of the Haitian.

Still worried about Miguel, he phoned Anita to inquire how he was doing. Very coldly she answered him by saying, "He is fine," and hung up the phone, before he could say another word. It was already late and night had set in. Knowing that Anita's parents would welcome him, even if Anita would not, he determined to stop by their house to see Miguel, when he finished his work for the day.

Just as he was finishing his paper work on the Dymphna Halloween arrests, Chief Conway came rushing into his office. From his demeanor, Forte knew that he had some breaking news.

"Look, Forte, I know you are anxious to get home, but there has been another murder. You have to go to investigate it. Monsignor Finolli has been shot at his condo. You remember some one tried to kill him there and shot a bullet through his hat. Well, this time he was not so lucky."

"Sure, Chief. I'll get on it at once."

His visit to Miguel would have to wait while he went to the crime scene behind Finolli's condo to where the homicide crew had already been sent. When he arrived, they were busy taking pictures of the corpse and preparing to put him in a body bag.

Forte examined the body. Finolli had the well-chiseled features of an American Indian princess. His Italian father had married a woman from the Lakota reservation. With his effeminate features their son Giuseppe resembled the mother. Even in death he still had the mysterious and sophisticated appearance that made him seem to be the perfect clergyman. He had been shot through the head with a 9 mm Baretta. Actually the bullet entered the back of his skull and emerged through his forehead.

"What did you find in the pockets of the deceased?" he asked the man in charge of the homicide team.

"A wallet with about a hundred in cash, his ID and a credit card."

"Is that all?" he inquired.

"All except a six pack of condoms with three of them missing."

Another priest to be remembered for taking a bullet in his head and having a half used package of condoms in his pocket. Wayne Creasy would have all the unsavory details in the morning edition of the *Rosanada News* and everyone would know that another priest had been unfaithful to his commitments. His heart heavy with sadness and discouragement, Forte watched as the crew zipped the mortal remains of Monsignor Finolli into a body bag and loaded them into the homicide van.

Although he was firmly convinced that Minimo Tabron and Gautier d'Arras were the murderers he was looking for, he now had to work another person into the equation. No doubt three men had been involved in the chancery murders—Tabron, d'Arras, and someone still unknown to him. He was still far from solving the brutal murders, but there was nothing more he could do until the next day.

As he listened to the radio in his police car to the news about Finolli's death, he drove to the home of Miguel's grandparents. He had always had a good relationship with Anita's parents and was relieved when they welcomed him into their home so he could see his son. Miguel was sound asleep as he tiptoed into the boy's room. Silently he stood by the boy's bedside and prayed for God to bless his son, keep him safe, and bring him and his mother back into the home he had made for them. Before leaving he bent over and very gently brushed his lips on Miguel's forehead giving him a good night kiss as he had always done ever since he was born.

As for Anita, she refused to see him, causing him

to leave with a very heavy heart and return to their empty house alone.

26

Forte

Sleep did not come easily to him, as he lay awake in his bed until long after midnight. A killer was still at large and he had no clue as to who he was. The only thing he had to go on was that the poison he found in Gautier's apartment was identical to that which killed L'Abbadon. About how it got into the archbishop's zucchetto and who put it there, he could only speculate.

When he finally fell asleep, he dreamed that Anita and Miguel had returned to their home with him and they were once again a happy family. She was again his beautiful bride that he had promised to love and cherish until death did them part. Just as he was taking her in his arms and kissing her, the phone jangled waking him with a jolt.

He glanced at his watch; it was three a.m. An unknown voice greeted him.

"Hello, Detective Forte?"

"Yes, I am Detective Forte."

The voice was silent for about thirty seconds, so he said, "Go ahead, I am listening. Who are you and what do you want?"

"This is Father Pompeo Dell'Anitra."

"Yes, Father?"

"You told me to phone you at any time, if I could give you any information about the chancery murders."

"Of course, I would appreciate any help you could give me. I appreciate your calling."

"I want to confess to being the murderer. Meet me in St. Dymphna's church in thirty minutes and I will give you a full confession, but I insist that you come alone. No cop cars and wailing sirens, you understand?"

"I am on my way and I will come alone."

Forte dressed quickly, drank a cup of instant coffee, and drove across Rosanada as fast as he could. It was a very dark night and St. Dymphna's appeared to be completely deserted when he arrived. Cautiously he climbed the warped steps that led to the entrance door, which he found unlocked. Shining his flashlight into the vestibule, he saw no one, and so he proceeded with revolver in hand to push open the swinging doors of the body of the church. Fear struck him as he glimpsed the statue of St. Sebastian whom he at first took to be a living man. Pointing his flashlight at the statue, he sighed with relief to see he was made of plaster, but shivered to see all the arrows that pierced his body causing him to drip with blood.

With his flashlight in hand, he glanced around the church. The statue of St. Dymphna holding her bleeding head onto the stump that was her neck unnerved him. When the beam of light hit the eyes of the demon she had on a leash, they glowed bright red in the night. Still he saw no one. Had he come on a wild goose chase? Had someone played a trick on him to get him to come here?

Drawing closer to the sanctuary where they had raped Jamie Shannon, he flashed his light upward toward the ceiling. A few bats began stirring. One broke loose from the rafters and began circling his head. He detested bats and swatted it with his hand. It was then that he saw something that startled him. Someone was hanging suspended from the rafters of the sanctuary, right over the altar. The body was still swinging back and forth ever so slightly. Forte shined the light on the face of the person who hung there. It was Pompeo Dell'Anitra. He had climbed up on the altar, fastened a rope to the rafters, and then jumped off the altar to his death.

After climbing up on the altar to try to determine if Dell'Anitra were by any chance still alive, he phoned for the homicide crew to come immediately to remove the corpse. As he was getting down off the altar, he discovered some papers lying there. Picking them up, he saw that it was a signed confession.

The homicide crew was there within minutes cutting down the body of the dead priest. The contents of his pockets proved his identity and provided them with the hand gun that he assumed was the one that had killed Finolli and Linde. He felt sure that the signed confession would explain why and how the murders had occurred.

27

Pompeo

Confession of Pompeo Dell'Anitra

I never set out to be a murderer, but I am one. I have killed five men in cold blood. When you read this, I too will be dead by my own hand. I do not make any excuses for what I have done, but I will try to explain what happened.

My half-crazy mother had eight children with eight different men. I was the youngest and never knew who my father was, except that he was a Mexican. Although she was never devout, she had me baptized Catholic and sent me to school with the nuns. When I was in my teens she converted to becoming a Latter Day Saint and married a Mormon. Her husband detested me and when the nuns encouraged me to enter a minor seminary, she was anxious to get rid of me and made arrangements for me to leave. I never returned home after that.

I was happy to be free, and although I did not like seminary life and did not have a vocation to be a priest, I stuck it out. I had no money, nowhere else to go, and no other way to get an education. I made a few close friends in the seminary. Minimo Tabron was one of them. He did not have a vocation either. He was strange looking—ugly and clumsy, had poor coordination, and was absolutely no good at sports. His legs were crooked and because of his lack of balance, he always walked as if he were half drunk. Nevertheless, he was my friend and I stuck by him even when he was in a mental ward for schizophrenia. Judging from the events at St. Dymphna's Halloween, his insanity has returned.

Excelling in academic work, I tried hard to become a good priest. When I was sent to Rome to study in the major seminary, I actually enjoyed the classes, but I found it difficult to agree with what they taught, and have maintained my own convictions to this day. Faith is something I have never had. Minimo has never had it either, but he was also a good student, and like me, had nowhere else to go. Because of his insanity I do not hold him responsible for what happened Halloween to Jamie Shannon.

I do hold the men I murdered responsible for their evil deeds. Although I have no faith, I have tried hard to keep my commitments of chastity and obedience. I would like to have had a wife and children and a home of my own. Instead I live in a home where the archbishop sends pedophile priests. I am not gay. Let me say it more emphatically. I am not a homosexual and I have never violated the virtue of chastity during all the years of my priesthood. Because some one with a criminal record accused me of sexually abusing him years ago, Archbishop L'Abbadon removed me from my parish, St. Giordano Bruno, and paid the accuser $125,000.00 to silence him. My accuser was not even required to swear out a deposition stating that I had abused him. The money was given to him quickly to silence him, because L'Abbadon could not go to court and defend me, because in doing so, his crimes would have become public. For years he has shielded pedophile priests and moved them from parish to parish, permitting them to keep on molesting young males.

Like me, L'Abbadon had no faith. In fact, I really believe he was an atheist. He lived in a mansion and wielded enormous power and could have put an end to the pedophile priests instead of just moving them from place to place. For years I wondered why he did not clean up the archdiocese. I finally learned his secret. He was gay and surrounded himself with other gays. As long as a priest kept his pants zipped up around young males, he left them alone. He always had a young priest living with him and on whom he bestowed great favors, far beyond what they had earned.

The night I killed Jan Zagan, I really wanted to kill L'Abbadon and hoped to get into his mansion and rid the Church of him. I had been secretly observing the archbishop's residence for some time and had found no way to gain admittance. I knew that Zagan often stayed there over night and liked to take a dip in the pool before retiring. The night in question, when I saw Zagan come from the archiepiscopal residence and head for the pool, I decided to kill him then and there and wait for a more opportune time and place to get L'Abbadon. I wanted Zagan dead, because he was the one who phoned me, telling me that I had been removed from my pastorate, and that they would never give me another parish. From everything I had heard of him, he was a fall down drunk that L'Abbadon protected as one of his old buddies. He had been a frequent visitor to Frankie's gay bar in years gone by, but stopped going there when he became vicar general. The night I killed him, I parked my car several blocks away and walked to the mansion and hid in the shrubbery. When Zagan entered the pool he was drunk and did not observe me. I snuck up behind him, jumped in the pool, and grabbed him, clapping my hand over his mouth. He was so drunk that it was easy to hold his head under water until he stopped struggling, for he was also completely out of shape. It was disgusting; he was even wearing a pair of L'Abbadon's shorts with the monogram CAL on them. I am glad I killed him. He deserved it. People like him are destroying the Church. He was just a bureaucrat who lived high on the hog. I thought it a stroke of genius and justice to cut off his penis and stick it in his mouth. It was so easy to kill him that I decided that night to get rid of all the gays in the chancery who were living dissolute and promiscuous lives.

I was still after L'Abbadon, but Stalker came next. He was easy to get. I hid in one of the public rest rooms in the chancery building late in the afternoon and bided my time. I knew that someone was in the archbishop's office working with him that night, but I was not sure who it was. I was planning to wait until the archbishop was alone and then go to his office and kill him. After I heard some one leave the building, I waited a few minutes and then went and knocked on the office door.

"Who's there?" a voice that I recognized as Stalker's called out to me. I then realized that L'Abbadon was the one I had heard leaving the building.

"It is me, Monsignor, Father Pompeo Dell' Anitra. The archbishop let me in the building, as he was leaving," I lied to gain access to his office.

Stalker believed the lie and let me in.

"What can I do for you?" he inquired.

"I wanted to discuss with you the possibility of my getting another parish assignment. I am totally innocent of the allegations that were made against me. I was not even in Rosanada at the time I was accused of sexual abuse. In fact, I was in Mexico."

Greatly annoyed that I had approached him, Stalker exclaimed with a fierce and penetrating look, "I really cannot be bothered tonight. I am very busy working on closing two parishes. You really will have to take it up with Monsignor Del'Ano. It is not my affair." He rose from the desk and started towards me to escort me from his office. It was then that I picked up the brass cigar lighter from the desk and smashed it down over his head as hard as I could. When I was sure he was dead, I slipped silently out of the chancery.

When I saw Monsignor Linde at Frankie's bar the night I went to the voodoo ritual in Gautier's apartment, I put him on my list of victims. He was wearing a gay pride shirt, holding hands with another male, and was obviously fascinated by him. When I killed him, I shot him with a secondhand gun I had bought at an auction. He was found with condoms in his pocket, two of which he had already used.

They expect us heterosexual priests to observe the strictest chastity. They told us we were not even supposed to look a woman in the face, because every woman was a womb waiting to be impregnated. However, the gay priests live with their lovers in rectories and do as they please.

Even though I had trouble trying to believe what they taught in the seminaries, when I went to school, they were still teaching what the Church has always believed. Now the seminaries are hotbeds of liberalism that do not believe the gospel and deny the real presence of Christ in the Eucharist. No wonder so many priests today have no faith and do not live moral lives.

I blamed L'Abbadon for the destruction of the Church in the archdiocese of Rosanada. I had to find a way to get rid of him. When I visited Gautier d'Arras in his peristyle, I knew I had found the way. Zombie poison was fast and deadly—1200 times more deadly than cyanide. When Gautier was busy with his voodoo ritual, I pocketed a bottle of the deadly poison that I had seen him use on a cat.

Once I had the poison, I kept waiting for an opportunity to use it. To make it a special event—one that would stand out in everyone's memory for years to come—I wanted his death to be a public affair in the cathedral. As the day for the consecration of Bishop-elect Bugumil approached, I conceived the idea of placing the poison in his zucchetto. It was easy for me wearing my clericals to go into the sacristy of the cathedral the evening before the ceremony and put the poison in it.

Naturally they brought him to St. Francis and I was the chaplain on duty who was supposed to minister to him. As he lay dying, unable to talk, but still able to hear my words, I told him that I was the one who put the poison in his zucchetto, that I was seeking retribution for all the innocent priests he had removed from their parishes and defrocked. I told him that his soul would burn in hell for his sins of the flesh that he was unable to confess in his mute state, reminding him that he was on the brink of eternity and facing the judgment seat of God.

I let Minimo entice me to St. Dymphna's on

Halloween. Horror filled me as I saw the bestial rape of the Shannon boy. Minimo is crazy, but the others had no excuse. When I saw Finolli like an animal sodomize the boy, I was enraged and went at once to my place and got my gun, came back to St. Dymphna's, watched for him to leave, followed him, and when he got out of his car at his condo, put a bullet through his brain.

All that remains now is for me to hang myself. When I was at St. Dymphna's Halloween, I saw the rafters over the altar and decided that was the place to end my life. Like Judas Iscariot, I have absolutely no hope. I have killed five men and am glad that I did it. I am the nemesis of those evil men who have done so much damage to the Church. Completely in despair, I am writing this confession to tell the world that I am the guilty party and that Minimo and Gautier are innocent of their deaths. I no longer believe in the Church, or God, or hell. I go now into that black night of nothingness from which there is no return.

Pompeo Dell'Anitra

28

Forte

Forte had made a few decisions and decided to discuss them with his wife. Having agreed to see him in the privacy of their home where they could talk freely just the two of them, Anita left Miguel with his grandparents and drove alone to rendezvous with him. He had done everything he could to make the house appealing, even putting fresh flowers on the dining room table. The food that he had picked up at the local deli was waiting for her arrival. He had bought the things that he knew she really liked—prime rib of beef, baked potatoes and roasted ears of corn with chocolate cake for dessert.

After they ate he would reveal to her his plans for the three of them, hoping that the nice dinner in their home would put her in a good mood.

"How's Miguel?" He asked as she came in the door. He had not seen the boy since Halloween, which had been a week before.

"He's fine and keeps asking about you."

"And how is Jamie Shannon?"

"He is recovering nicely. I talked to his mother

on the phone just this afternoon." She took her place at the table.

"This is lovely. Fresh flowers and even candles on the table."

It was good news that Jamie was doing well.

"What did Mrs. Shannon say?" he inquired.

"She told me that he is even more determined to be priest than before all this happened. He insists that he is called to be a holy priest and to make reparation for the bad priests who hurt him."

"Amazing!" he replied. "God's grace is truly amazing. All things are possible with Him."

"The dinner is delicious. Thank you."

"My pleasure," he said warmly. "I am glad you are enjoying it."

Knowing how much she savored it, he had brought a bottle of Chardonnay and poured some into her glass. He was delighted to see that she sipped it eagerly.

"It could have happened to Miguel," he said, "if I hadn't gotten there in time. He could have been next. They already had him deeply drugged. Thank God I got there in time." Forte shuddered in horror at the thought of what might have happened to their son.

"Yes, I have thought about that too," Anita replied.

"Well, I have made some plans that will help us improve our situation," Forte confided hoping that she would be receptive.

"What do you have in mind, Cristian?"

"I have decided to go to law school and become an attorney—to become an officer of the court—like my dad. I want to defend the innocent, and if I can become, in time, a prosecutor and put criminals behind bars. I have always been a bit of a crusader." He waited to see her reaction to what he had just told her.

"That is a wonderful idea! How exciting! When you become a lawyer, you won't be out investigating homicides at night, will you." She paused and thought about it for a few moments and added, "I will be proud to be the wife of an attorney who is a crusader for law and justice." She jumped up from her chair, came over and threw her arms around him, as he put the chocolate cake down on the dining table. Giving him a big hug, she asked "Do you mind if I spend the night here tonight?"

About the Author

Son of an American mother and a Spanish father, Josue Raul Conte, a native of Andorra, a principality in the Pyrenees, was born in 1969. After his early education with the Jesuits, he enrolled at the Opus Dei University of Navarra in Pamplona, Spain where he received his doctorate in medieval philosophy and literature. During his years at the university, he became a member of the Neo-catechumenal Way, but later was very disillusioned with the stringent constraints of ultra conservative Catholicism and adopted a more moderate approach to his faith and left the Way. Having taught a various colleges and universities, he is now a free lance journalist, living in San Francisco with his second wife Alicia and Ivan, their Russian wolfhound. He is also the author of *The Stones Cry Out!* and *Rosanada Requiem* that continue the story that began and complete the Rosanada Trilogy. For more information visit **www.contebooks.com**.

www.ingramcontent.com/pod-product-compliance
Lightning Source LLC
Chambersburg PA
CBHW020323260626
47156CB00004B/1357